AFTER THE GREEN WITHERED

KRISTIN WARD

After the Green Withered

By Kristin Ward

This is a work of fiction. Names, characters, businesses, places, events, locales, and incidents are either the products of the author's imagination or used in a fictitious manner. Any resemblance to actual persons, living or dead, or actual events is purely coincidental.

Independently Published

Editing: David Taylor, thEditors.com

Cover: JD Cover Designs

ISBN: 978-1982900731

To my husband,
Who could've predicted that stopping you in the high school hallway would've led to this grand adventure? Now that would be a good story to tell!

And to my boys, who believe in me.

PROLOGUE

We've all heard the stories of how it began, but no one really knows the truth because no one ever owned up and took the blame. Anyone who was there when it all started is long dead and all that remains is their awful legacy. All I know that is real, true, is that the world wasn't always like this. It used to be green.

I suppose the awareness of a looming crisis began slowly, perhaps with a faucet that ran dry or maybe a water restriction where there had never been one. Whatever it may have been, there was a turning point and from that moment on the United States of the past disappeared under a burning sky.

. . .

This is what I have come to understand of our history, that thing buried and skewed under hidden agendas and untruths...

In the early 21st century, the voice and face of the country changed. An exploding population triggered an energy crisis that swiftly grew beyond our borders and enveloped the world. Wars erupted over control of these dwindling energy sources, resulting in a recession that dwarfed the crash of 1929. Our nation's leaders responded by doubling down on efforts to extract resources in every forest, ocean, and watershed, rather than investing in what many viewed as 'unproven technologies'. Companies that specialized in advancements in sustainable energy were forced into bankruptcy, halting the tide of progress. Environmental protections ceased to exist as everything from national parks to the once pristine Arctic disappeared under an onslaught of drilling and mining that left these places barren and poisoned. Coal, oil and gas burned, unchecked and ignored. The results were devastating.

Massive storms, brought on by rising temperatures, began to dominate newscasts. People watched as violent hurricanes in the Indian Ocean destroyed whole communities, washing away thousands who had been unprepared for the force of the waves. The eastern seaboard saw Category Five hurricanes on a monthly basis, until many areas became uninhabitable. But the drilling continued.

Extreme weather escalated, as tornados ripped through areas in Europe and Asia that had never experienced the phenomenon before. In one night, Hautmont, France was wiped off the face of the earth as a previously inconceivable F6 tornado spent twelve minutes on the ground. And yet the event was soon forgotten, the majority of citizens preferring stories of scandal and entertainment and war.

As the climate grew hotter and drier, the last of the ice caps melted belching out methane trapped for millions of years and filling the ocean with too much fresh water, creating a chain of unfathomable and merciless events. The Maldives disappeared under the sea, followed quickly by other island nations across every ocean. Tens of millions of people were left homeless in places like Japan, the Netherlands and Bangladesh, as huge swaths of land became submerged, leaving many cities uninhabitable swamps. New York City was inundated with tides that never receded. While Florida became a ghost of its former self, as millions fled the water-ravaged state.

The desalination of the oceans, combined with high levels of acidity and rising temperatures, took effect. Beached whale species, from dolphins to orcas, became a common sight. Coral reefs died off on a global scale, looking like bleached underwater graveyards. Fishing communities went bankrupt and prices for seafood skyrocketed until only the very wealthy could afford it. The ecological imbalance further poisoned the already toxic oceans, making even the technology to convert salt water to fresh water for human consumption only possible for the elite. And still, the refineries continued to process their crude oil.

The sixth mass extinction event in Earth's history continued. Species from insects to mammals died off at unprecedented rates, unable to acclimate to changes that occurred in years as opposed to centuries. The few remaining rainforests saw these extinction events on a massive scale and those species unlucky enough to need polar climates were gone after a few years.

Precipitation continued to dwindle while massive dust storms swept through towns and cities, choking the air and causing havoc for those stuck in their midst. The city of Las Vegas experienced a storm of such intensity that the sky turned black as sand and dust covered every road and building, until the metropolis was buried under a layer of dirt that took months to cleanup. While in the western half of the country, wildfires ravaged California, displacing thousands and turning huge swaths of land to smoldering ash. And through it all, fingers of blame, rather than solutions to the root cause, became the norm as scientific evidence was censored.

Drought continued to creep across the world, silent and ruinous.

Initially, the areas hardest hit by drought were underdeveloped countries. Starving children or withered remains of cattle splashed across the screens in the living rooms of U.S. citizens who, though saddened by the images, remained ambivalent. Most people viewed the water wars raging in Africa or the battle over rights to the Amazon River, with a sense of detachment. But there were some who voiced their warnings, pitting themselves against the majority, fracturing the nation.

Environmental activists attacked refineries and shipping lines, disrupting the flow of resources to such a degree that they were labeled terrorists and hunted down by the government. Those who took a pacifist approach did no better at conveying their message, as their forewarnings were mocked and disregarded as hippie ideologies by those in power. Eventually, messages of the resistance were defined as alarmist rather than credible, making them easy for people to discount. All the while, areas experiencing water restrictions grew. But most citizens saw these measures as nuisances, rather than portents of worsening problems. This perception would not last.

It was a global drought of unprecedented proportions that cared nothing for which hemisphere you lived on nor how much money you held in your bank account. Over time, even the staunchest disbelievers were faced with undeniable truth. Emergency measures to curb the effects to the US were taken and hope stirred in the minds of the populace. Those technologies that were shuttered in the early days took on new life in ambitious plans for fusion power plants and hundreds of square miles of solar panels and wind turbines. Rumors of unmanned spaceships launched into the solar system to find a new home and escape from our dying planet, circulated throughout the country. But time eroded such fantasies and reality crushed those hopes, as years turned into decades that saw no relief from the storm of devastation. The efforts were simply too little and came far too late.

Eventually, our nation's borders closed and all refugees were turned away, no matter their circumstances or family connections. Those citizens made homeless by severe weather migrated, desperate and angry. The land itself began to wither and no part of the country was left untouched by the unrelenting scarcity of water.

After several years, rain became a fairy tale for children to imagine. The aquifers, which provided water for the breadbasket of the country, dried up. Crops shriveled while the nation spiraled into chaos. Food shortages became common and soon starvation and civil unrest were rampant. Those starving children and dying cattle were no longer relegated to the problems of 'other countries'. Parents struggled to feed their families, further driving people out of their homes in a frantic search for food and water. This brought out the ugliness in human nature that you only see in times of desperation.

A militarized presence emerged as violence became pervasive. Riots and looting led to lottery systems for food and water. This method ultimately failed, as seen in cities like Houston where a small war erupted and obliterated the landscape. States threatened to secede. Fearing a nationwide revolution, the president took extreme measures to preserve the majority of the country. Hawaii and Alaska were stripped of statehood, being too remote and damaged by rising seas and economic catastrophes.

The remaining lower forty-eight states were restructured to eighteen, each representing a unique river basin. This reorganization was aimed to prevent states from entering periods of civil war over water rights as each state now had its own water resources. Borders grew along these new lines, complete with heavily guarded checkpoints to keep the influx of destitute people from pouring in and overtaxing an already untenable situation. Towns followed suit as entire communities were abandoned. Soon it became apparent that to live outside a regulated community meant death. Survivalist factions arose in opposition, but were dealt with, swiftly and severely. The country became unrecognizable.

Not everyone had ignored the signs of catastrophic problems. In the shadows, one group led by a visionary man named Oren Frey, had seen an opportunity and quietly took control of water resources from reservoirs to real estate above aquifers. When things began to look desperate, this agency, The Drought Mitigation Corporation, offered their assistance in distribution and long-term water usage. Under the leadership of an impotent president, the DMC's power grew, while the pillars of democracy became more divided and vulnerable. By the time the DMC was fully entrenched, the drought had taken the lives of millions and changed the face of the country forever.

I LIVE IN THE AFTERMATH.

MY MEMORIES OF CHILDHOOD ARE PLAGUED BY water, or rather the lack of water. Laundry sitting in a dry wash tub or covered in dust on the floor. Food containers we have to scrape and wipe down with a towel so they never really get clean. Dirt that never leaves the underside of my fingernails because washing my hands is not always an option. Dust storms that roll through and leave behind a coating of grime on every surface, even the inside of my nostrils. And then there are the nightly, televised announcements of civil wars, border violence, and rationing. These are the images and realities of my life at seventeen years of age because, by the time I was born, water was the global currency.

It wasn't always thus
This tragic world
Of dust and death
But the green withered
And with it
Our dreams for the future

CHAPTER ONE

Life, as it is...

The siren blares. It is six o'clock in the morning. No one should have to wake up to the scream of a siren at this hour. But it's Tuesday and they always go off at this time on Tuesday. I groan and roll to my side, pulling my pillow over my ears. As if I could forget what Tuesday means. As if anyone in this town could. I sigh after the noise stops and flop onto my back. There is no use trying to get any more sleep. I need to get up in thirty minutes anyway.

Tuesday. Tuesday means no water in my community of Prineville, in the Pacific Northwest Basin. No flushing toilet. No washing hands or hair or anything, for that matter. It means standard-issue antibacterial lotion that chaps my skin and gives me a rash. It means that I have to brush my teeth with a dry toothbrush and let the spit sit in the sink alongside Mom and Dad's. It means piles of dirty dishes because we can't wash plates and silverware. I better use my leftover water ration wisely.

I stretch and face the inevitable task of getting up and starting the day. The relentless sun is already beginning to shine through the cracks in the shades, causing the temperature to begin its daily climb to a point where light films of sweat will pool on my skin, triggering my body to lose water that it can't afford. I walk to my metal dresser and pull out a pair of standard issue, threadbare shorts and a shirt that has only a few stains. I dress and sit on the edge of my bed to plait my hair, the best style when it's not quite as clean as it should be.

In the bathroom I lean into the mirror, under the blinking of the harsh bulb that has never quite worked right, and check my face for any pimples or gunk stuck in the corners of my eyes. Finished with the inspection I gaze at my reflection for a moment, taking in the dirty blond hair, pale blue eyes, and smattering of freckles sprinkled across the bridge of my nose and cheekbones. I will never be considered a beauty. My eyes are too small, my face too narrow. I sigh and head to the kitchen.

Our modular always feels claustrophobic in the morning. Like my bedroom, the shades are kept closed as often as possible to block the sun and keep the house cool, though by late afternoon it feels stifling regardless. My dad is sitting at the table, the only seating area in the home, cradling a mug of stale, synthetic coffee while his mind is elsewhere. Like all adults that I know, his skin is thin and wrinkled from too much sun and not enough moisture. I stare at the painfully dry and cracked skin along his knuckles where he grips the mug. His hair, once a dark blond like mine, is peppered with gray and thinning on the top so that I can see the pink of his scalp through the sparseness. I wave my hand in front of his face.

"Hey, Dad. You in there?"

I often find my parents in this state. It has gotten worse as I have grown older and at times I worry that one day their eyes won't flicker back to life.

"I'm sorry, sweetie, I was wool-gathering. Want some?" he asks as he holds up his cure for morning fatigue.

I shake my head. I've tried the stuff but it tastes like crap and doesn't give me any energy anyway. Instead, I go to the pantry, grab the last breakfast ration, heat it up in the microwave, and join my dad at the table. We sit in silence for a few minutes, the scrape of my fork the only sound, until he seems to shake off his stupor.

"Only a few weeks left, right Enora?" He's referring to my graduation from high school.

"Yeah, just a few weeks."

I don't bother adding anything more to the conversation. Graduation is not something I like to think about. It is this inevitable milestone that is coming closer to becoming a reality that I am afraid to face. My dad doesn't seem to notice my lack of response. He is back wherever he had been when I found him.

Soon my mom shuffles in, her feet making a sound like sandpaper rubbing against a plank of wood. She is dressed in a uniform of slacks and a matching, unflattering shirt that balloons from her body like a sack. Both are pale blue as opposed to the darker shade of my Dad's clothing. Like my father, my mom's age is evident in every line etched into her sour face. I think that she must have been pretty once. Perhaps her blue eyes sparkled with youth years ago or maybe she smiled often. Now though, she is dried up and resentful. She mumbles a hello, grabs a mug, pours a cup of the lukewarm sludge, and plunks herself down at the table, which tilts precariously on its uneven legs before I grab the edge and right it. Mornings are quiet in my house.

I am an only child. That is all that is allowed. Couples that wish to have a child must apply for a license and after passing a series of genetic tests are given permission to become parents. Every now and then you hear rumors of those people who have bucked the system and had a second child. Those stories never end well.

We sit in silence until a low rumbling permeates the house as a shuttle pulls up to the end of our street. This is followed by a message that flashes on the wall screen alerting my parents that it is time to board the shuttle. At this point, my parents lift themselves from their chairs, give me a perfunctory kiss on the cheek, and head to work. Knowing they'll be working gives me some relief, at least they'll earn some credits and, looking at the nearly empty cupboard, we need all the credits they can earn today.

My parents are paid in water. Not literally of course. Rather they are paid in water credits. It's not just us either. The entire country uses water credits as currency. It is highly regulated and portioned throughout all eighteen states and there never seems to be enough. Honestly though, I can't imagine what my life would be like if water wasn't controlled. People don't always make the best choices and if it were up to us, letting that faucet run unchecked wouldn't seem like a big deal. We'd likely be suffering severe dehydration if our supply wasn't shut off when we met our quota. It's all about control for us, from the wall screen to the water credits. Everything is regulated and nothing goes unnoticed.

As I sit alone in the kitchen, I stare down at a slightly raised lump, barely visible under my skin. This is their form of regulation in its strictest sense. Inserted into my arm at birth is my key to survival in the community. Everyone has a microchip on the inside of his or her left wrist. It is our permanent identification and so much more. Anytime we need to buy something we slide our arm into the reader, which scans our code, and credits are debited from our family account. The opposite happens when my parents work. For each day of work, credits are put into the account. Our microchip isn't only used for our water credits though. When I get on the school shuttle, arrive at the school or even pick up my lunch portion in the cafeteria, I am scanned.

The Company's database regulates everything as we are scanned throughout the day. That's what we call them, the Company. It's really the Drought Mitigation Corporation or DMC. They have been in charge since before I was born. No one knew about them back in the early days of the drought, or so my dad once told me. People found out later and by then the DMC had control of all of the water in the country, but the power they had was really much greater than that. Now they have stations outside every town and systems that regulate water rations, usage and credits.

My parents don't particularly like the DMC. While my Dad's views of the Company are rather moderate, he sees some of their controls as invasive. He can often be found mumbling about this or that, but is generally apathetic. Mom is much worse. She is constantly berating the Company and refuses to see the essentials of their actions. I've stopped engaging in debates with her, it's a pointless effort. I may not like the DMC, but I understand the role they play. If it weren't for the rampant waste of previous generations, things would be different. But this is the world I inherited.

Everyone is on water rationing in addition to our water credits. To regulate water usage, each housing unit is monitored and when the threshold is reached, the water is shut off remotely so that even in those times when we have enough credits, we have to wait. Everybody has rainwater drums outside their homes on the off chance that rain will come. But those days are so rare that the drums are dry as a bone most of the year. Inside we conserve as much water as possible. We even have a small pan under the bathroom and kitchen faucet to catch any drips that may fall because, you never know, there may be enough for something as mundane as rinsing your hands.

As I said, on Tuesday there is no water. Every town has a day when the Company shuts off the water to help conserve it. This has always been the way. Clearly, that doesn't make it any easier. I feel bad for families with a young child. It must be hard to listen to the cries when the water runs dry and the ration is used up. In my housing section, it's not so bad. I think we have all gone to each other at one time or another for a bit of water. I can't say the same for other housing sections or other towns.

Like most people, we can rarely afford to buy our full water ration, always enough to sustain our bodies but never enough for the many other uses that require it. Most of our credits go toward food although the credits don't go far. Meat is the most expensive, which means we rarely eat it. I've seen pictures and videos of cows, but the amount of water and resources it takes to raise one means it's a luxury families like mine can't afford. Instead, we usually buy the DMC meat substitute. I'm not entirely sure what it's made of and, honestly, I don't really want to know.

In addition to control over the water, the DMC grows and supplies all of the food. They have farms, specially designed greenhouses, and processing plants across the country, which produce everything we eat. Their greenhouses are huge buildings with the typical solar panels that we all have, lots of glass windows, and intricate water recycling systems that minimize water waste. They have stockyards and fields of crops too. As expected, these compounds are heavily guarded. My parents have told me stories of earlier years when these locations were often raided and food was stolen. That doesn't happen much anymore, thankfully. In school, I've only had to watch one broadcast of the execution of one of these traitors and I have no desire to ever see another.

I SIT ON THE GROUND JUST OUTSIDE MY EMPTY HOUSE, waiting for the electric sound of my shuttle and once again contemplate how we got to this point. Not just me. Everyone. The whole world is affected by a drought that really should be called something different because it has been going on for about a hundred years, globally.

I feel the heat on my skin and look up hoping to see a bank of dark clouds rolling in, but as usual, the sky is clear. No rain for me. In school, they tell us that during the wet cycle of the earth this part of the country is a lush landscape of green where the trees are healthy and a clear day is a rarity. I wish I could see that. I can't imagine a world of green.

In history and science classes, we're taught about the reckless fossil fuel and water usage of the past and how the DMC stepped in to protect our future. If not for the Company putting a stop to the drilling and then investing in renewable energy sources, the sky would be a blackened, sickly thing. As for water, in my time wasting water is not something we do. It's too precious. To waste it is a crime for which, even my parents, would want consequences. Of course the DMC control goes far beyond water, but without their intervention things would be even worse.

In Prineville, the forests hardly resemble anything even remotely green. With the drought, most of the trees dried up long ago and then bugs moved in to finish them off. The only trees that are left are scraggly, drought-resistant things that dot the land around town in small clusters. In the footprint of the old forest just inside the perimeter of town, there is now just a graveyard of trees lying on the ground, like dead soldiers in a war with no enemy.

I don't like to visit what remains of the forest. It's too quiet. I find myself wondering where the animals went. Did they die too? Are their bones buried deep within the cracked earth?

I find it hard to breathe sometimes, everyone does. It's

like the air is somehow depleted or has gone so bad that my body tries to reject it. Most days it doesn't bother me, but there are times when I begin to wonder if my lungs are working too hard and will up and quit. It must be the lack of trees or the dust in the air or maybe something noxious they don't tell us about.

Local history class taught me that a century ago this area was a large lumber community, which I find hard to fathom. I do know that the town was much larger and sprawling than it is now, you can see the proof of that beyond the fence where the old buildings sit vacantly. Those parts of Prineville look like a ghost town, eerie in their emptiness. I just find it hard to imagine this place as some thriving environment where the forests were so lush that trees could be culled and sold for wood. It's so different now.

Due to the loss of the timber industry, wood is unaffordable and, as a result, the few remaining original houses in Prineville are worn down, old things with sagging roofs and peeling paint. No one can even live in them anymore and I wonder why they don't tear them down. Nearly all of us live in modular homes. They look like cubes when viewed from the outside. Square windows with rounded edges are the only things that break up the bland structure aside from the front door. Each residence is made out of a synthetic material that wears better under the blistering heat than an organic material ever would. Still, most of our homes look like they have seen better days, having become faded and covered with dust over years of living.

Every neighborhood is set in an organized grid with a specific type of dwelling. There are eight neighborhoods in my town, Sections A-H. Most families are located in sections E-H, mine being section G. A family unit has two bedrooms while single or childless housing have only one. The only part of Prineville that could be considered nice is near the town square where you'd find the families of the Sentinels living in sections A and B. These modulars are larger and newer with the latest interactive screen systems and furniture made with cloth rather than the hard, artificial material the rest of us are stuck with. But I'd rather live in my section. The Company may be great and all, but at least here I can be myself.

A FEW STREETS OVER I HEAR THE FAINT WHINING OF my parent's shuttle as it picks up more passengers. It always makes me shudder when I hear it. Like most families, my parents work just outside of Prineville's border in the textile mill. Many of the residents of Prineville end up working in the mill, as jobs are scarce in town. Kids get such glamorous choices as: working one of the menial jobs in public utilities, working at the textile mill, getting shipped off to a larger manufacturing facility with housing, or getting recruited. The scarcity of employment options means most of us end up slogging through life in jobs that will never extend beyond the tedious. With the DMC bringing in all of the goods we need, local craftsmen are obsolete.

This is one of those things that get under my Dad's skin, forcing his turtlehead to emerge from his hunched shoulders as he fumes about how things could be better without the DMC controlling all facets of production. I guess he has a point about how the Company has made innovation among the populace a thing of the past. He often refers to my grandfather's time during these rants, reminiscing about the old days when local craftsmen and independent businessmen were common. My grandfather was one of those successful businessmen, owning a company that employed hundreds of workers. Apparently, he was one of the elites when things got bad. People with money always seem to do better, even now that's true. Yet his money only took the family so far and now we are just like the bulk of the population in my town.

When my dad rants about how things in the past were better, I find it hard to bite my tongue. I want to just yell and say that if the ways of the past were so great, then why did grandpa's business go belly up? I mean, I wonder if my dad even realizes that the he's lucky to have a job from the Company. If he works, then it means we're not left to someone else's mercy. His job at the mill may not be much in terms of personal fulfillment, but it keeps our family from homelessness.

Our mill produces the synthetic cloth that is used for

uniforms for the DMC and is the primary employer. I really don't want to end up at the mill. I don't want to come home with an aching back, chapped hands, and the dull look that I see so often in my parents' eyes. Geez, now I sound like my Dad. It's hard to look toward the uncertain future.

If I lived in the past, I could have moved to a different town or even a different country, but not now. The drought caused so many mass migrations of people that all of the states closed their borders, and when that wasn't enough, cities barricaded their populations behind cement walls and larger towns absorbed the smaller ones putting up fences to build their own borders. The populations in these refuges were untenable and viruses and scarcity took their toll. Now we are stuck. The only time you can leave is for work at the mill or if you are recruited by the DMC.

The barbed wire fence surrounding my town is patrolled twenty-four hours a day. I have been close to the fence a couple of times with my friends, when we've talked jokingly about running away, about sneaking through the border and getting out, finding a place where water flows, clean and free. But the guards carry large guns, and besides, it's just talk anyway. We all know it's nothing but desert out there.

It could be worse. On the evening announcements, they always show how awful it is in the big cities, like Brigford, all of the violence and food shortages, viral outbreaks and choking air. We are told that it is like this in every large city across the country, though it must be beyond imagining in places like Chicago where overcrowding is the norm and violence is rampant. My parents say that it is better we live in a small town. For once, I have to agree with them.

CHAPTER TWO

The shuttle to school arrives. It is an ugly, electric thing. A relic from bygone days, with wire mesh embedded into the windows and hard, plastic benches that my legs stick to as I sweat through the seat of my shorts. To me, it has always seemed like some kind of transportation for criminals, although traitors caught by the Company have always been forced into vehicles much newer than this one. Still, it feels oppressive and considering where it takes me each day, I guess that's appropriate. Reluctantly, I hop on and scan my arm before finding a seat. The trip is short, as my house is the last stop before the school. It's an old, two-story building with cracks in the brown walls and broken tiles on the floors. Very little new construction can be found in town and fixing up the school is not a priority.

As a twelfth-year student, in just a few short weeks I

will turn eighteen, graduate, and begin working, beginning my contribution to the community. I try not to think too much about this but it is always there, at the back of my mind. Sometimes I feel like school is such a waste of time since I know there are few real choices for where I will end up. My teachers would argue that by getting my education I am better prepared for the workforce, but I hardly see how deconstructing a sentence is going to help me work the loom at the mill or drive the truck that picks up recycling from residences. I almost wish that we were not given any options, simply placed in our early years in the track to which we will be assigned for the duration of our adult lives. If everything were predestined like that, then I would never have to go through this uncertainty. Of course, that idea sounds great now, but in reality, I'd probably hate it even more. But being thankful for my limited choices isn't how I'm feeling as I travel closer to the school. I don't want to end up bitter and angry like my parents, but it's hard to see the positive and as much as I hate to admit, I can understand their resentment.

I suppose the dynamics at Prineville High are typical of any high school. There are popular kids, I call them drones, who live in the newer section of town. All of these kids have family members who work in the militarized branches of the Company. They have newer clothes and aren't scraggly wraiths like the rest of us. It's a common sight to find them ganging up on the kids who don't seem to fit in anywhere. I don't trust the drones. They are too perfect, like they are all cut from the same genetic material. It creeps me out, hence their nickname.

The remainder of the student body is like me. Most of us are on the hungry side wearing our standard issue clothes that have patches or holes because there aren't enough water credits to buy new. I only have a couple friends. Well actually, just one now, who is the sole person I can be honest with. I guess you could say that I'm not really the social type. The idea of entering a room full of people I don't know is about the worst thing I can think of. If I could sit outside in the shade with an actual book, instead of a Company-approved text, and not have to talk to anyone, I'd be in my own version of utopia.

As the shuttle pulls into the lot, I see my friend, Safa, standing outside the school entrance looking for me. Safa and I always head into the building together, though our schedules allow us to share only two classes. She is the one bright spot in an otherwise dreary day filled with people I equally loathe and avoid. We greet each other and she begins to chatter about her latest project. Safa always has some crazy project she is working on.

As she begins a verbose explanation of her current obsession, my mind starts to flip through the many 'projects' that she's designed in the past. I smile to myself when I get to her biggest debacle.

We were ten years old and Safa's fixation at that time was pottery. We had just learned about ancient people and had been shown different artifacts, like shards from clay pots and utensils made from bone, from those cultures. Safa decided she wanted to create a vase out of clay that future people would find, thereby learning about our time in history. Naturally, clay was not something that family credits could be wasted on even if we could have found any at the supply depot. So, Safa decided she would make some clay herself.

The biggest problem with making clay was having any water to mix with the hard, packed dirt in her yard. This challenge was mulled over for a couple of days until Safa decided that water could be substituted with her parent's synthetic coffee. To back up the use of such a liquid, she had determined that the ingredients she used to make the clay would be additional information for future people to interpret.

I can remember that afternoon like it was yesterday. Safa gathered up her dirt and coffee and placed it into a pot on the stove so that it could 'cook' which would make it more durable. Looking back on it now, I suppose I should have stopped her from putting the airtight lid on the pot. The noise made when lid blew off was enough to make us scream and run into her bedroom, slamming the door behind us. When we finally gathered up enough courage to open the door and creep into the kitchen, the mess splattered on every surface was truly astounding. Not having any spare water with which to clean it, we scrambled to find old cloths to wipe away the most obvious blobs before they hardened. Needless to say, if you look closely at the cracks between the cabinets and those in the floor, you can still find remnants of it to this day.

While I have been reminiscing and half listening to the hum of Safa's voice, I stop mid-stride when I hear the word "*garden*" come from her lips.

"Are you crazy?" I nearly shout.

"Sssh," she says and looks around to see if anyone is listening.

Safa pulls my arm and hauls me into an alcove in the hall. "Don't talk so loud. I don't want one of the drones to hear you!"

I lower my voice. "What is wrong with you? Don't you know what can happen if you get caught?"

She rolls her eyes. "Look, I'm not waving it in front of everyone's face like those idiot neighbors of yours did. I'm being careful."

Planting our own garden is strictly forbidden. The rationale that we are told is that planting our own food wastes water resources, but I think it's more than that. The Company regulates this law with frequent sweeps through town. My neighbors were caught a couple of years ago with a tiny garden hidden in an old rain drum beside their residence. They had planted some tomatoes or something. I remember being jarred awake in the middle of the night by a loud noise. I looked out the window and saw guards from the Company hauling my neighbors out of their house and into a van. Their residence was empty by the end of the week and a new family moved in. We don't try to grow our own food. Besides, our own efforts would probably waste too much water or be totally inefficient anyway.

"Safa, they didn't flaunt it either. It was hidden in a rain drum and they still found out." I can feel the speed of my heart ratcheting up a notch.

"You worry too much," she says and swats my arm. "Look, you have to come over and check it out."

I shake my head. Inside I'm thinking, what if I get caught?

"Come on," she whines. "Please?"

And then she gives me the eyes, the ones that translate into: *If you were really my friend you would do this for me.*

So I cave. "Fine. But I swear if anyone finds out..." I don't finish the thought because, really, the answer to that is not something I want to explore.

"It'll be fine. See ya at lunch."

She gives me a quick hug and jogs to class. I stand in the alcove for a few more minutes, telling myself to calm down and stop worrying. After all, we're just kids anyway and it's not like they are going to do anything to a kid.

I PASS THE NEXT FEW HOURS OF THE SCHOOL DAY either listening to a mind-numbing parade of monotone voices lecturing from the front of the room or from the headphones that are becoming more common in each class. I loathe the headphones. The sound invades my senses and is inescapable. But I have a suspicion that the headphones are not going away any time soon. After all, with the DMC talking in my ears, teachers can't tell you something they shouldn't.

It's a woman's voice droning in my ear this period. While my mind wants to wander, I find it impossible to ignore the information pouring into my head.

"People of the past were incredibly wasteful with their resources. An average citizen used over a hundred gallons of water each day. This was not sustainable as the earth's weather changed."

I've heard this statistic countless times, as though they are trying to drill it into my head. I wish I could tell them there is no need to remind me of the recklessness of past generations. Just hearing the idea of a hundred gallons of water being squandered by every person in the country is enough to rouse my anger and resentment.

"Some organizations tried to curb this excess, but their efforts were ineffective and the waste continued. It wasn't until the Drought Mitigation Corporation, or DMC, got involved that lasting structures were put into place to safeguard water for future generations. In order to protect this essential resource, the DMC took control of public and private water sources. This ensured that every citizen had equal access to water.

Your town once had multiple water sources like wells. Those that remained after the initial dry-period were drained by the DMC and transported to a treatment facility. The refined water is distributed based on the number of individuals in each household and the availability of credits toward water for non-essential purposes. In this way, all members of a town receive the water needed for survival and multiple everyday uses.

In the early days, not everyone embraced this revolutionary thinking. Insurgent groups grew in pockets throughout the country. These rebels were responsible for numerous attacks on facilities, supply lines and branches of government. The worst of these attacks occurred in Phoenix, located in the Great Basin. A group of rebels targeted branches of the DMC, preventing any warning to the public, while devices were strategically placed in varying locations. At a predetermined time, this terrorist group detonated bombs at DMC facilities across the city. Over fifty thousand people, DMC employees and civilians, died as a result of this attack."

My eyes flick to the screen that lights up showing the devastation. The photos are a reminder of the cost of war. The entire class is glued to the images scrolling across the screen, many of us leaning forward to see the details in the wreckage of collapsed buildings and twisted hunks of metal. A collective gasp reverberates around the room when the first human casualty is splashed onto the screen. The shock turns to horror when a photo of what may have been a schoolyard floods our eyes. There's not one person in the room who isn't affected by the image. Even the drones, whose snarky comments peppered the first few pictures, grow silent.

After the last image is shown, the narrator continues. "The DMC is here to protect you from this kind of devastation. Through government coordination, we can prevent future acts of war and the senseless loss of life that is seen in countries across Europe and Asia. We need your help to ensure the safety of all civilians. By graduating and entering the workforce, you have the opportunity to help safeguard our way of life for future generations."

Following the video, we are assigned a reading passage about the Phoenix attack and the subsequent measures that went into effect to protect the populace from rebels launching future assaults. I glance around the room, taking in the faces scrolling through their personal screens as they absorb the information. I can't help feeling like what I am reading is a bit one-sided and I wonder what the intent of the rebels truly was. Were they making a statement? Was the attack an effort to regain control of resources? Had they been attacked first? These questions are not answered as I read. I guess they aren't important anyway.

A bell rings and I stand up to head for lunch. All of this is so much to take in. The world was so different before. I find it hard to imagine it. As I slowly make my way out of the room, a drone shoves past me, knocking me into the doorframe. Typical. I don't matter in their eyes. I know I should be used to it but it pisses me off regardless and I'm tempted to say something to him. But I keep silent.

The only time I really surface from that inner place I go when in class, and actually speak to someone, is during lunch. I walk through the lunch line, picking up my measly ration. A few kids ahead of me is Ariel, yet another one of the lucky ones whose father is some kind of bigwig at the DMC training center. I can't help noticing the food on her tray, it looks so much more appetizing than my globs of mush that I know will stick to the roof of my mouth as I struggle to force it down. My mouth waters as I see her reach for an orange. There have been a total of five times in my life that I have ever tasted the incredible sweetness of that fruit and each time it was only because a friend, with more credits than me, shared a few slices. Bram was always doing things like that.

I shuffle forward with my unappetizing meal, place my arm in the scanner, and then survey the room looking for Safa. She is seated at a table in the corner of the cafeteria and waves me over. As I make my way through the maze of students, I notice that Safa is not alone at the table, which unfortunately means we will have to censor our conversation when all I really want to do is grill her about this idiotic and dangerous garden idea. Lunch passes too quickly and too soon I find myself with headphones on and the Company talking in my ears again.

By the end of the school day, my anxiety over the garden has returned. I skip taking the shuttle home, meet

Safa in the back of the school, and we begin the long walk to her neighborhood in section E of town. She is positively glowing, bouncing around and telling me about how she thinks she's discovered this new way to cultivate food with very little water. So little, she says, that everyone could have a garden and wouldn't it be nice if we could all grow some of our own food? Just mentioning water makes my mouth feel parched and I consider taking a few precious sips of my ration. But I squelch the thought. The idea of giving even a few drops of the precious liquid to a plant is slightly appalling. I'm always thirsty and would rather every drip of water coats my tongue, keeping the pervasive cottonmouth at bay.

I listen to her prattle on but inside I am a ball of worry. All I can think of is what will happen to my friend if the Company finds out. I don't share my worry. I know she won't heed it anyway. Safa has always gone her own way, justifying her actions with this and that. The heat of the day beats down on my head as we continue our trek. The billboards we pass, usually easy to ignore, catch my eyes today. Things like, 'We are all responsible for protecting our resources. Report water wasters,' and 'Notice something unusual? Report it and keep the community safe. The DMC is here to protect you.' I feel a strange compulsion to turn Safa in when I see these reminders and it fills me with self-loathing. I am not an informant.

We arrive at the house and she hauls me through the front door, not where I had anticipated going, and into her room. Like most family modulars, there are two utilitarian bedrooms, one bathroom, and a small kitchen with room for a table. Like mine, space is cramped but livable and it's nice to have a small pocket of the house to ourselves. Safa's parents are still at the mill and won't return for another hour so there is no need to keep our voices down or be discreet.

At first, I don't notice it. It's much smaller than I had imagined. In truth, I actually don't know what I had imagined, just not something that would fit on the shelf under her bedroom window. There is a thin, clear plastic tarp over it and I can see drops of water that have collected on the underside of the plastic.

"Here it is!" She announces proudly. "Want to know how it works?"

I have to admit that I am curious. Being so small, it is hardly the threat that I had imagined earlier and now I am beginning to consider the possibilities.

"Yeah, definitely," I say with a grin.

I sit on the bed as she uses her hands to explain how she has managed to grow a small garden in her room with very little water. So little, in fact, that her parents haven't noticed an effect on the water ration nor have they seen the contraption in her room. As she explains how it works, I study the garden more closely. The small plants don't even sit in soil; rather they are planted in gravel that I can see is made up of rocks Safa has found. Their thin roots are visible snaking through the cracks in the rocks, which are sitting in water. The container itself is covered with transparent plastic that looks like it had been packaging material from a box of protein cubes. I can see droplets of water collecting on the underside of the plastic that will eventually become so heavy they drip onto the plants. It's ingenious and yet so simple.

As I take a closer look a thought pops into my head. Where did the seeds come from? You can't just buy seeds in town. I mean, why would you need them if you're not allowed to plant a garden? Plus, any fruits or vegetables that we buy have been genetically engineered to be seedless. That means only one thing.

"Safa, where'd the seeds come from?"

I see her eyes dart away and then she mumbles, "I just got them."

"From who? I mean it's not like you can just buy them at the repository?"

"I can't tell you. I just got them, okay?"

She has started wringing her hands and I know that if I push it she'll cave and tell me who it is. But do I really want to know? Didn't someone once say, ignorance is bliss?

I sigh. "Okay, I won't ask. But I'm worried, you know? I mean if someone else knows about this then it just makes it riskier."

I know she gets it and I hardly need to point it out, but I'm scared for her. What if she can't trust this person who supplied the seeds?

"I know you're worried, but it's already done so there's really nothing you can do now anyway."

I let out an exasperated breath. "Fine. I'll ignore the seeds, but what about the water waste? You shouldn't be using your ration for this. The small amount of water we're given means that every drop counts and being so wasteful is going to hurt you and the community."

Safa looks at me and rolls her eyes. "Oh my God. I can't believe you just said that. Sheesh. You sound like Mr. Frink. He's always spouting DMC bullshit."

I make a face at the comparison. "I do not sound like that little automaton!"

"Yes, you do!" Her voice rises before she takes a calming breath and continues. "Here's the thing. The Company facilities that we learn so much about have like a twenty percent water waste. My design recycles all the water and none of it ends up being wasted."

I must look confused because Safa pulls me closer so I can see what she's talking about. "Do you see any water from the top and sides of the dome that end up on anything other than plants or the rocky soil?"

I lean in. "No."

"Well the Company has greenhouses for water recycling and they tell us that eighty percent of the water they use is recycled. That means that twenty percent is wasted. If they used my design then they would save more water."

"Hm." I think about what she's said. In science classes we've heard all about various food operations, but I vaguely remember statistics about recycling and water waste. Obviously, Safa paid much closer attention than I did if her numbers are accurate. "I get it."

"Good. So you see how mine is more efficient? I mean, if each family used this design then everyone would have more food, better tasting stuff too."

I nod, thinking about the lunch I choked down. I imagine I can still feel the lump slowly moving down my dry throat. It would be wonderful to have fresh vegetables and fruit that I could eat anytime I wanted. Maybe if the Company did find out they'd see her design as an improvement on their own production techniques and Safa wouldn't get arrested. The shred of hope gives me some ease as I make my way to the edge of the bed to sit down.

She sits next to me and we both just look at her illegal garden. It's magnificent in its simplicity. But despite its cleverness, it's the biggest threat I have ever known.

Other than a quick, conspiratorial wink at the lunch table the next day, Safa and I don't mention the garden. It's our secret, a small thing we hoard that is tucked within the tedious normalcy of school. I do admit that I am worried. It's not like I can forget that what she's doing is against the law, but I like to think that the Company wouldn't see her creation as a complete violation of their rules. They're not out to get us and Safa isn't some water traitor or anything. In fact, she hasn't even used any more water than what she's allocated. That would certainly count for something.

The day drags on and though my niggling worry is there, my mind wanders to the larger concern in my life, leaving school and entering adulthood. I know my days are slipping away and that I will need to choose among my limited options, but the choices are all equally unappealing. I feel like I'm being funneled into a life I don't want. To be fair, every job is necessary to the community but I just don't see myself being happy here knowing what is available for most graduates. Being a Sentinel, or working in a similar position at a DMC headquarters, is not something I want either. Those jobs may mean more credits, but I have no desire to end up like the people I know who come from rich families. I don't want to end up like a drone.

My eyes roam the faces that surround me in the classroom and I wonder how many other minds are drifting down the same road. How many others are fighting an internal battle? Maybe if I really put a lot of effort into my placement exam I could end up out of this town and see a bit of the world. That would mean working for some specialized branch of the Company but, as long as it is far from a military role, then I would do it.

After school, Safa and I return to her house to unwind. Hanging out in her room, a once normal activity, feels a little different now as I take furtive glances at the garden.

"Why do you keep looking at it?" Safa asks after a particularly long look.

I shrug. "I can't help it. It's just...I don't know. It's kind of scary I guess."

She rolls her eyes. "Enora, you need to relax. Nothing is going to happen, okay? Besides, with all these crazy regulations the Company is just asking for people to take things into their own hands. It's not like they'd be surprised that some of us are fed up with how things are."

I huff, a little offended that she thinks I'm some unreasonable worrywart. "You act like this is no big deal, but it is."

Safa shakes her head. "Look, if it makes you feel better, then I promise I will stop with what I have now. I won't get any more seeds and I won't make this any bigger or anything. Okay?"

I feel slightly mollified and say, "Thanks. You know, I just don't want you to get caught or anything."

"I know, Mom!" She nudges me hard and a small giggle escapes as the seriousness of the situation evaporates and I let go of my unease.

Soon our conversation drifts to other, less critical things and I let go of all of my angst over the events in my life. Safa helps me to do that, just her presence works to lift my spirits and lets me know that at least one person gets me. There used to be another who understood all that I am, but he's gone now.

CHAPTER THREE

A week later I am sitting in my science class when I hear a message over the loud speaker and through my headphones.

"Enora Byrnes, report to the recruitment office."

My heart drops. I can feel a sea of faces staring at me with expressions of shock, pity, and even envy. Mr. Frink hurries me along and I find myself in the hallway walking toward the recruitment office. I can hear my every footfall echo off the walls. The *clop, clop* sound of my shoes reverberates through my body like the ominous toll of a bell. I reach the office door much too soon and with shaking hands open it to my future.

I enter the room quietly and give the secretary my name. She is expecting me. I am told to have a seat while she informs the recruitment officer that I am here. I lower myself into an orange, plastic chair in the waiting area and begin to take slow, deep breaths in an effort to calm my racing heart. For the first time, in so long that I can hardly remember, I feel cold. Not the type of cold that can be fixed with a jacket or warm blanket, the type of cold that seeps into your bones, radiating throughout your body until your muscles shudder. I feel sick.

Being recruited by the Company is not something I would have envisioned for myself. I am not strong or smart like the drones I have seen handpicked over the years. There is nothing about me that stands out as one who would make a good candidate for Sentinel or whatever role they see me filling. But no one refuses a recruitment assignment. So when I see the shiny black boots peeking out beneath the hem of a black and gray uniform, I raise my eyes and know that there is no choice. For whatever reason, I have been selected and this will be my future.

The recruitment officer has a nice smile and warm brown eyes. He doesn't look much older than me but I can't remember seeing his face on the school grounds before. He is not the one who makes the recruitment decisions, but he is the first step in my transition. Inside my head I am begging that I haven't been slated to become a Sentinel. I don't want to become one of the uniformed guards who patrol the streets, borders, transportation lines, food processing facilities, or repositories.

"Enora," the man reaches out his hand. "It's a pleasure to meet you. I'm Chad and I will be your first contact in the exciting journey you are about to begin. Won't you come this way?"

I follow Chad into a small office and sit as he shuts the door. "I'm sure that you are eager to learn all there is about joining the DMC team. Let's start with your placement exam."

He shuffles through a small stack of papers in a file, looking them over. I can see various graphs and numbers but am unable to make out what they refer to. "I see that you scored very high in a couple of areas. Your visual acuity is phenomenal as is your software aptitude. Those skills could lead to an interesting career in the field. Have you thought about what branches of the DMC you would like to pursue?"

"Um, I'd like to see the world a bit and would enjoy working in a food production facility or something like that." I sound so lame but am unprepared with a specific job title.

"Hm. Those are great options and are important aspects of the support the DMC provides to citizens, but I think you might find that your particular skills lend themselves to a more rigorous assignment. It is very likely that you could become a Sentinel. You could even find yourself in a large city, thereby seeing more of the world." He smiles at his assertion while I cringe a little inside.

"For the time being," he continues. "We are going to place you with the other recruits who show a strong propensity for traits we look for in Sentinels. These students will be familiar to you, I'm sure."

Of course they'll be familiar. I've always made it a point to be aware of the drones, it helps me avoid them. "Yes, sir. I am sure that I will see some faces I recognize."

"Excellent!" Chad replies. "Over the remaining weeks of the school year, you will begin your journey with the DMC by attending specialized classes during and after the school day. In addition to this..."

His voice becomes a murmuring in my ears and I find myself incapable of grasping what he is telling me. I look around the room, unable to fathom why I am sitting here listening to my potential future as a Sentinel being laid out before me. This is not me, but how do I tell this man who sits before me explaining the honor and benefits of working in this capacity? I bite the inside of my cheek in an effort to refocus and listen to what he's saying.

Chad begins to explain the first step in the recruitment process. And then he is standing, holding out his hand for me to shake.

"It is a pleasure to invite you into our ranks, Enora."

My hand is cold and clammy as I take his. "Thank you, sir."

In the waiting room, the secretary stops me and gives me a stack of papers to take home. A couple of them are colorful brochures. One shows a group of smiling Sentinels and citizens greeting each other at a checkpoint. Another contains images of food and water being distributed into the hands of children and young mothers. I look again at the grin of the Sentinel and try to imagine myself in that role. But he looks like every other drone I've come across making the picture seem fake. My parents should be happy. For them, working as a Sentinel means more credits. These employees earn more than those who work at the mill. It isn't fair, but that's how it is. To my folks, this'll mean a better life. But for me, it means something different.

Two years ago my closest friend, Bram, was recruited. He was a couple of years ahead of me in school and was at the top of the class. I remember his face so clearly, though it has been so long since I have seen him. Before the recruitment, I could look into his brown eyes and know that he truly saw me, understood who I was under the layers of indifference. He had a rugged profile, chiseled and handsome, though boyish at the same time. I used to crane my head to look into his face and scold him for ignoring me or laugh at his stupid jokes. I miss that.

Many of my fondest memories of childhood are of the two of us, just playing around and having fun. Bram and I spent many evenings together, sitting on a hill behind the old library. It was our favorite spot. We weren't supposed to go up there after curfew but if you knew the hidden paths through the dry shrubs and buildings, it was pretty easy to sneak on up without being spotted by the

Sentinels. And considering the number of ears that could potentially listen to conversations at school or in town, it was the best place to be able to really talk. Every now and then, Safa would join us but most nights it was just Bram and me.

From the bald spot at the top of the hill, you could see the whole town spread out before you, and in the dark, it almost looked beautiful. At least with only the pale light of the moon, you couldn't see the scarred landscape and dilapidated buildings that are so evident under the harsh rays of the sun. We always kept to the edge of the clearing, out of range of those that might scan our location. Most nights were spent dreaming of a different future, imagining things that we could only read about or hear of. Every dream we wove into the canvas of our minds, had us together and living lives away from this place and the hardships that it represented. Truth be told, each fantasy also included bodies of clean, clear water and torrents of rain that would wash over us, wiping away the worry along with the dirt.

Not all conversations were of an unattainable future though. Many were candid dialogues about our realities. The looming threat of graduation was the central focus of our last few encounters because, for Bram, that future was getting steadily closer. I remember the look in his eyes when Bram would talk about the recruitment that he feared was an unavoidable conclusion to his eighteenth year. They didn't look scared, just...empty. Like the spark for life was gone from them already, though no decision had actually been made.

I recall him looking into the dark horizon saying, "I feel it in my bones, Enora. Like at any moment, I'll get called down and told that I've been recruited."

The conviction in his voice hit me like a hammer, shocking me so that I blinked slowly, trying to dispel what he said and the future it represented. Bram just looked at me and waited for me to process what he'd said.

"You're going to be one of *them*? A Sentinel? You're sure?"

I tried to temper the accusation in my tone, but the flicker of anger I saw on his face let me know that I wasn't successful. "I'm sorry, that came out wrong. I'm just...it's just..."

"I know. It's not the future we imagined, is it?" I shake my head. He didn't really need to say anything more, just opened his arms and let me slide into his embrace.

As he held me I remember thinking how unfair it was. Bram shouldn't have to suffer worry over recruitment. He shouldn't have to be taken away from me to the training center to be instructed as a Sentinel. It's a place I can't and don't want to imagine. To me, the center is the last stop before you are turned into a soldier for the DMC. The graduates from this program have always been a part of my life and they represent one thing about the Company that I have never been able to fully support. Too many times I've witnessed these chosen few push others around and use their strength and weaponry to intimidate. That's why only the drones are supposed to be chosen. They are the ones who seem to thrive on keeping others down. Bram can't become one of them.

We had such grand plans once, or at least we talked about such grand plans. He was the only person who really understood me; it was kismet with Bram and I. And now he's telling me that he thinks he'll be taken away, to become something we both abhor.

I shook my head against his chest, refusing to accept this prediction. "No, you can't be recruited. You're not gonna be a Sentinel, it's just not who you are. I mean, you're not some kind of drone or something. You're going to end up like me, a pleb cleaning out toilets and scrubbing floors."

He chuckled. "Toilets, huh? I don't think so. I think I'll let you take care of the crap and I'll take care of the floors."

I elbowed him, glad that the seriousness of the conversation was derailed. "Fine, have it your way. But at least make sure we're on the same shift, would ya?"

Nothing else was said about his misgivings that night, nor the next few that followed, and I chose to ignore the potential truth of his fears. It was easier to pretend we had all the time in the world. But Bram wasn't able to push away his worry so completely.

In the following weeks, I saw him less often. Our secret meetings on the hill became infrequent, as though he were preparing himself. It was like he began to cut me out of his life that night and slowly removed me from his heart until I disappeared from it completely. After graduation, Bram was taken to a training center outside of town. The last time I saw him, he was carrying a gun and the boy I knew was gone.

I don't know what happens in training. No one who has been through it ever talks about it, at least not to me. Bram was the only recruit that I had been friends with who was chosen because most of those selected run with a different crowd. They are brawny soldier types, perfect Company material. But not Bram, he was different. He and I used to talk about escaping all of this and finding a life beyond the border, we had such dreams. But it was just talk and now it's not even that.

THE REST OF THE SCHOOL DAY PASSES IN A HAZE. I don't recall walking back to class. After school I see Safa waiting for me to walk home together, but I sneak past her and hop onto the shuttle. When my parents arrive, I am sitting in the dark at the kitchen table with the papers from the DMC scattered before me. When my mom's eyes fall onto the table, she gasps, turns to embrace my father and falls into his arms sobbing. I get up and shut myself in my room.

CHAPTER FOUR

The rapid integration into recruitment begins immediately and time passes quickly as the end of the year races to a finish. Three weeks go by in a blink and I haven't seen much of Safa. Not since the recruitment. I've just been too busy. This must be part of the transition as my class schedule was changed after the initial meeting, offering little chance of mingling with anyone who I may have been friends with prior to being recruited. This doesn't affect me though as I don't socialize much anyway. Outside of school, I have been required to go to orientation meetings with the fourteen other recruits. I meet with Chad, and the other recruits, daily. I feel like the Company is starting to erase my previous life and instill a new one. It's hard to admit, but it's not so bad really.

The meetings I attend each day are filled with various

histories and overviews of the Company, things they don't teach you in regular classes. I learn that when our water sources were becoming a problem in the early 2000s, the DMC got a government contract and helped them find ways to conserve and recycle water. They set up different collection and distribution centers that we still have today. Without their support, the government probably would have spent *years* wasting water. Eventually, the DMC's role grew as the country was faced with everything from food shortages to huge numbers of people moving from places that were too drought-ridden. It was actually their idea to form states based on river basins. The Company helped our country get through the scariest time in history.

Today, the DMC uses their control to keep our whole population safe and ensures that we have enough to live on. One of the sessions I go to explains the importance of this role and how all of the recruits are going to help keep these things going and make sure everyone is safe.

Chad explains, "In order to ensure that all citizens are provided for, the DMC has calculated the amount of water that each of us needs, for both survival and daily uses. This information helps the Company provide for each family while also making sure that there will be enough for future generations." He pauses and glances at each of us. "This task is not easy. You have all seen newscasts of water traitors attacking distribution lines and facilities. Your future role may be focused on preventing these incidences. I'm not going to lie to you and tell you that being a Sentinel is easy, but it *is* necessary. If not for certain positions, like those protecting supply lines, rebels would steal as much water as possible, either hoarding it or wasting it. Can you imagine the cost if we did not protect our resources?"

I can picture families, like mine, being left on our own and I wonder how long we would last. It makes me angry that there are people who are hell-bent on disrupting the very things that keep every person alive and cared for. There seems to be an underlying selfishness in the acts of these traitors. I admit that being assigned as a Sentinel could be a good thing.

I hear Chad resume talking. "The DMC helped our country survive the greatest natural disaster in history. Without this assistance, it is possible that millions more would have died as a result of the drought and lack of serious conservation efforts. Now you will continue to fulfill their vision, preserving and protecting our future."

We all nod, as this statement is one we embraced early on in our meetings. It is impossible to disregard how essential the DMC was in preserving our way of life. One of the other recruits, Mica, raises his hand. I suppress an irritated sigh. Mica is always feeling the need to open his big mouth and share something, even though most of what he says doesn't really add to the conversation. He just likes to hear himself talk. "I think the DMC did more for our country than our own government."

As usual, another recruit gives Mica a big high-five. I

want to roll my eyes. There is little camaraderie for me as I sit in these meetings. Unlike Mica, I don't blather on for the sake of hearing myself talk and I sure don't get or give any high-fives. I am one of them and yet, I am not. These are drones, born and bred for this life. What am I? Where do I fit in? I understand and accept the importance of my part in this, but I still feel like such an outsider. I'm literally the outlier in a room full of kids who've known from infancy that they would be recruited and serve in some military capacity. This is the one part of this whole transition that I struggle with every day.

I sit quietly, as usual, while Chad continues. "I agree with you Mica and appreciate your perspective of the DMC." Oh my God, now the drones are giving each other back pats. It's almost too much. But I don't let my less-than-complimentary thought bubbles out.

"As you have learned in your various science and history classes, the US was not the only country that suffered from drought in the early days. The crisis actually began in Africa and South America. The countries in these continents did not know how to deal with the rapidly growing droughts they faced each year and, over time, millions of people died as a result of their inability to put things into place to protect their resources. Of course the DMC offered assistance to the most heavily affected countries immediately, but were refused. Sadly, this refusal had catastrophic effects for their citizens.

When the successful measures taken in the US

became apparent to the global community, countries from around the world reached out to the DMC and contracted with them. In this way, the support of the DMC was felt in every pocket of the world."

They are global? I had not known this, although based on what Chad has said I'm not surprised. This is one of the many things that only the people in this room will learn. Those selected for recruitment by the DMC learn its full history and, as a recruit, I have signed a statement that assures them that I will keep confidential any information that I gain. To do otherwise would result in repercussions not only to myself but my family as well. It makes sense to have this layer of knowledge passed on to those of us who will have important roles in the Company. If I'm being asked to fight for something, it's only right that I know what that something is.

I refocus my attention as Chad stands and picks up a poster-sized paper. "As you can imagine, being a global corporation, the DMC needed to design a symbol that truly represented their essential role and was recognizable by the public." He turns the poster around and I look at the emblem I have seen throughout my life. "All of you have seen the DMC logo, but do any of you know what it means?"

A couple of unsure hands rise. As expected, Mica is called upon first. "Does it have something to do with water?"

Chad smiles. "Yes, there is a part of it that does mean

water. After all, it is the scarcity of water that started it all. The DMC logo has three distinct parts. The triangle represents earth or land. Over this shape is a horizontal line that signifies water. The vertical bar indicates power. In essence, the symbol stands for power over land and water. It is this control that has enabled us to survive."

I look at this common symbol in a new light as Chad wraps up the meeting. The deeper meaning of each part of it makes sense to me. I acknowledge that there must be someone looking out for all of us, someone who can make the choices that people, as individuals struggle to accept and carry out. Someone has to assume the position of power and responsibility for the masses.

As we leave our session, Lina, one of the other recruits, asks me to hang out with them at Mica's house. I can't help a spasm of shock crossing my face. I've never spent any time with the drones outside of these meetings and admit that I'm both curious and excited at the prospect. I follow the group onto the street and walk among people I've seen shove misfits to the ground because they walked too close or mock kids whose clothes were so worn they sported holes. These are not kids I have ever wanted to emulate, but I admit that it feels pretty good to be accepted. Of course, I also feel a sense of guilt. Safa and I have always scorned these people. It seems like a betrayal to befriend them. I decide to ignore my conscience and enter Mica's house with a sense of belonging.

. . .

Vaguely, I know that Safa is worried as the days go by and we see little of each other. She has come by the house a few times. But I find that I can't explain what's happening, not even to her. She doesn't like the Company and refuses to accept that they are necessary. I mean, without them we'd probably be dead. But I can't tell her this. I don't want to start another argument. So I keep quiet about everything I'm learning and talk about normal things.

Safa seems to understand that my recruitment is a subject that can't be broached. She knows me so well and accepts that we see things differently in this way. So we just sit and pretend that nothing has changed.

During one of our conversations, she fills me in on her illicit garden and the anxiety I feel for the risk she is taking is there, but strangely muted.

"You should see the plants, Enora!" Her excitement is bubbling over, typical Safa. I smile, although it comes out crooked. "Aw, come on, you can do better than that!"

I can't help but chuckle. She's always known how to get under my skin, past the defenses and quietude.

I roll my eyes, lean forward and with exaggerated enthusiasm say, "Oh my God, did you say plants? If you tell me you've got a frigging tomato growing already I'm gonna pee myself!"

She laughs. "You're such a pain in the ass. I don't know why I put up with you." Safa bumps me playfully and I pretend to fall over.

We sigh at the same time, then giggle, and for the first time in a while, my worry flutters away like leaves tumbling in the wind. Her eyes sparkle as she describes how well the plants are growing and that she even has her first vegetable beginning to flower, though it's not going to be a tomato.

As we talk, the time passes and soon the conversation turns from the garden to me. "I miss you, Enora."

"Yeah, I miss you too."

It's hard to talk to Safa about how I feel about this abrupt change in the direction of my life. My insecurity is always there and I'm almost afraid to feed it by letting it out in conversation. But I also know that I have to be able to talk about it, even if it's just being able to share a few things. Safa knows this too and I imagine she's just been biding her time, waiting for me to be ready to open up. So I keep it simple and tamp down the anger.

"You wouldn't believe the classes I have to go to. It's all about the Company and how great it is and all. Plus I'm stuck there with all the drones, I feel like a total misfit."

Safa nods. Our dislike of the drones has always been common ground. Well it was until very recently, but I ignore that truth for now. "I gotta admit that I was pretty shocked when I found out you had been recruited. I mean, it's not like you're the usual Company material, no offense."

"No, you're right. I thought the same thing, which is why it's been really hard. But I'm stuck, right?"

I look at her face, gauging her reaction and hoping she'll see some of the benefits that I do.

"No one says no to recruitment," she mumbles. "But hey, at least you're gonna get out of here and see the world, like you've always dreamed. I'll probably end up at the mill."

"Nah. You'll find a way out." But I don't really believe that and neither does she. We let the idea sit there, a small lie that reflects the divergence in the paths our lives may take.

During the last week of school, I am fitted for my uniform and on graduation day, I wear it for the first time. As I stand in front of my mirror, I can hardly believe that the image is real.

Is that *me*? I look like a drone.

The slacks are black with gray striping along the seams of the legs. The shirt is also black with two gray stripes that begin at the hem and flow over my chest and down my back to disappear under the waist of my pants. These are the nicest clothes I have ever worn. The only color aside from the relentless black and gray can be found on my sleeve, blood red and bold - the DMC logo. You can find the logo on anything that comes from the DMC and now I am wearing it, as though I too am produced and owned by them.

As I continue to gaze into the mirror, I note how my face has filled out a bit, making me look less angular and softening my cheeks. The increase in family credits, since my recruitment, is showing. I've seen it in my parents as well and though my mom is reluctant to admit any appreciation for the Company, I've heard a few comments here and there which tells me she does.

As soon as the ceremony is over, my parents join me. My Dad wraps his arms around me, telling me how very proud he is and how he knows I'll do great things. My Mom is less enthusiastic but that's just how she is. I see Safa lingering beyond my parents. She's smiling and trying to catch my eye. I'm about to go to her when Lina comes over and pulls my arm. She starts to drag me toward the other recruits who are whooping in excitement.

As we go past Safa she calls out, "Enora!"

Lina looks over at her and snidely replies, "She doesn't have time for you, pleb."

It hurts to see the comment sink its teeth into Safa.

Her gaze swerves to me and I see betrayal wash over her face when I say nothing. Not even after Lina asks, "You're not still friends with her are you? She's a nobody."

I don't reply. I just let my body be propelled toward the crowd, leaving Safa behind.

Rain falls upon the earth
Washing away
The traces of you
They are like the rain
Sweeping through me
Until I am gone

CHAPTER FIVE

My parents don't see it as goodbye. They give me hugs and wish me well, but not goodbye. They are secure in the knowledge I will bring with me a better life, an easier life.

To me, it is almost like a funeral. I will leave my life behind when I board the shuttle to the training center, a two-hour drive. As I'm about to climb in, I take a look around, hoping to see Safa. I don't want to leave without apologizing for ditching her after graduation. It wasn't right and it's been eating at me ever since. But she is nowhere to be found. I sigh and face the shuttle.

I fully take in the mammoth transport. It is the vehicle to my future and the symbol of my break with the past. Taking a deep breath, I step inside. This is the first time I have ridden in such luxury. I feel a flow of cool air wash over me as I walk up the short steps and make my way to plush seats that sit next to tinted windows. It makes our school shuttle look like something that should be relegated to a vehicle recycling plant.

I settle into my seat, enjoying the cushy softness, and I look out the window. I see my parents. My Dad has his arm around Mom. It looks like she's been crying and I feel a pang of sadness as I watch them. They'll be alone now and will be moved into a childless unit since I'm moving on. At least it will be in the better part of town. It is unlikely that I will see this place again. The only way I might is if I'm stationed here as a Sentinel or something.

I realize that I'm heading toward a future I did not choose and may not want. I feel like a drone as I look down at my sleek uniform. I am just like the rest of the recruits now and am a bit fearful of what that may actually mean. Will I end up like those Sentinels who harass people at the border, using their power to intimidate? Or will I be able to withstand the influences around me and retain the part of myself that is compassionate and human?

As the shuttle pulls away, I watch my parents wave goodbye. The electric motor whirs as we head down the road and Bram's image slips into my mind. The one time I saw him after his training, he was a shell of the boy I knew. Sure, he was there, standing in front of me, talking. But he was gone. There was nothing of what made him, *him*. It was like who he was had been sucked out and replaced by a stranger. I don't want to lose myself.

As the shuttle continues, I gaze out the window

absorbing whatever peace I can through the sights of familiar places. I know that I may see these things again. Training isn't forever and if I am lucky I will get a post in town. This should console me, but it doesn't. I feel as though being stationed here isn't a realistic option.

My neighborhood passes by as the shuttle makes its slow progress, and I try to take mental pictures so I can conjure them up when I'm feeling the inevitable loneliness of the training center. As we come to the edge of section G, I keep my eyes on Safa's house, a place of countless happy memories.

I watch as her front door flies open, having been kicked from the inside by a Sentinel whose hands are occupied with Safa's struggling form. A cry escapes my lips as I watch her forcefully pulled from the doorway and dragged a short distance toward the curb. I start to pound my hands on the window while yelling, "Safa!"

She can't hear me and I watch in horror as her parents pour out of the house following a second Sentinel. Safa's mother runs and grabs the arm of the man holding her daughter, trying to pry him off. The second Sentinel shoves her backward and into the arms of Safa's father, who is yelling as he catches his wife. I can't make out anything they are saying over the low hum of the shuttle, but I see Safa turn to the man holding her arms, tears streaking her face as she mouths something to him. As the man responds, I see her father launch himself at the other

Sentinel who pulls out a baton and strikes him on the side of his head.

Safa's father stumbles, hands holding his head, and then lands on his knees. Her mother, horrified, presses her hands together and pleas with the Sentinel who holds the baton menacingly in the air, like a cobra ready to strike.

"Safa!" My voice is getting hoarse and I realize those around me are trying to pull me away from the window. I hear Mica yell at someone to shut me the hell up and then Lina is there telling me "Calm down, Enora. Your pleb friend is just getting what she deserves. She's probably a water traitor anyway."

I ignore Lina and keep my focus on the scene playing out before me. I see Safa elbow the Sentinel holding her arms, who loses his grip. She bolts to her father, but before she can get to him, the other Sentinel snatches her mid-stride. He twists her body around so that her back is to his chest and propels her forward.

When Safa plants her feet and refuses to budge, the Sentinel loses patience and shoves her so forcefully that her body is thrown forward onto the ground, face hitting the cement so hard that blood and broken teeth splatter the pavement.

All I can do is pound my hands on the glass screaming her name as shuttle moves on. All around me are exclamations of everything from: "Did you see how her face smashed into the ground? Sentinels are so badass!" to "I can't believe Enora even associates with that girl. What's her problem anyway?"

I don't even feel it when Chad injects a sedative in my neck, everything just goes dark and I am gone.

After the shuttle arrives at the training center two hours later, I am carried off and removed from the other recruits, though I have no memory of it. I spend my first night in the infirmary, sleeping off the drugs and hysteria. First thing the next morning, I am escorted to an interrogation room.

It's a small space with a metal table and three hard, plastic chairs. The gray walls seem to be closing in on me as I sit in the empty room. The only thing that breaks up this monotony is a poster of the head of the DMC Intelligence Agency dominating a wall. General Malvolia stares at me, her eyes hard and frozen. It's an image I've seen before but today it feels ominous. I try not to look at it.

I'm not sure how much time has passed when the door opens and two men walk in. They are wearing unfamiliar uniforms so I know they aren't Sentinels. They sit down opposite me and introduce themselves.

"Enora, my name is Agent Sinclair and this is Agent Banks. We would like to ask you some questions about an incident that occurred yesterday."

I try to gulp but my throat is so dry that my spit gets caught halfway down and I have to cough to free it. The men stare at me like I'm an insect and wait for me to pull myself together.

"Let's get started, alright?"

I nod.

"On the shuttle, you became upset by an incident that was occurring out the window. Is that correct?"

"Yes." I reply, trying to keep my voice steady.

"What can you tell us about that?" I see him move a recording device closer to me. I feel threatened by its presence.

"I only know what I saw."

"And what did you see, Enora?"

I look at both men but there is no understanding in their gazes. "I saw my friend dragged from her house and thrown to the ground. She was hurt badly."

"Do you know why she was arrested?"

"No." I'm so scared they will see the lie.

"Didn't you just say she was your friend?"

My nails dig into my palm. "Yes."

"How is it that you didn't know about her illegal activities if she was your friend?"

"Illegal activities?" I let my brow crease in feigned confusion. Inside, my mind is racing. I know it's the garden they are referring to. Or at least I assume that it is. But I can't let on that I know anything about it. If these men were to find out that I kept this secret then I'd be just as guilty. My parents would probably be accused of covering it up too.

"Your friend is facing some serious charges." It is Agent Banks who has made this statement and I watch as Agent Sinclair leans back in his chair, letting Banks take over. "She's a water traitor. Are you trying to tell us that you didn't know?"

"I don't know what you're talking about. A water traitor?" My voice sounds small and I force myself to sit up straighter.

"In addition to being a water traitor, she has also been charged with violating our cultivation laws."

"I don't understand." My heart is racing as these crimes spin through my brain. The last water traitor I heard about was executed. I remember watching it at school and listening to the subsequent lecture on the detrimental impact these traitors have on our society.

"Your friend violated two of the most serious laws in the country. These laws safeguard our resources. Do you understand the seriousness of this situation?" Agent Banks puts his arms on the table, shifting his body forward so that his eyes bore into mine.

"I understand the laws, sir, but I don't know about the crimes you are saying she's guilty of."

He sits back. "I find that hard to believe."

I clear my throat, having chosen an excuse that may work. "I haven't really seen Safa for weeks. Ever since my recruitment, I've been too busy."

Neither man says anything but I watch them glance at

each other in silent communication. Agent Sinclair eventually says, "I understand from your recruitment officer, Chad, that you have had a rigorous few weeks. He informed us that your attendance and participation were exemplary."

"I am thankful to do my part. I've learned a great deal about the importance of the DMC." I can see from their expressions that what I'm saying is having the desired impact. So I go for the clincher. "If I had known Safa was a traitor, I would have reported her myself."

My statement mollifies the men. "And you would be right to do so. Being vigilant is everyone's responsibility."

"Yes, sir. Traitors hurt the community and I would never support one." I feel awful. *Oh Safa!*

They both nod, pleased with my response. "If you recall anything of significance over the next few days, you will report to us. We are in the process of gathering as much information as possible so that we can find all of the traitors involved in this situation."

I am unable to stop myself from asking, "What's going to happen to her? Safa, I mean."

Agent Banks looks sternly at me. "That is none of your concern."

"Yes, sir."

I'm dismissed, having passed their 'truth test'. As I get up to return to the infirmary for a brief health assessment, Agent Sinclair says, "We're interested to see your progress through the training program, Enora."

It's a threat. They are no more interested in me, than I am in them. They'll be watching me. It's as simple as that.

A Sentinel shows me into the recruit dorm and points to the location of locker room with showers and toilets along with the sleeping quarters. After the quick tour, I find myself in a large room with rows of bunks stacked on a cold, hard floor. After setting my bag on my assigned trunk, I sit on my bed and replay the images of Safa being ruthlessly struck down. I don't bother to stop the tears from falling, I need to get it out and no one is here to witness it.

Why was she dragged out like that?

How could they charge her as a water traitor?

I thought I was coming to have a deeper understanding of the DMC, but now I begin to wonder and worry. Am I going to end up like that Sentinel who threw her to the ground?

I replay the scene of her face hitting the pavement in my mind until my eyes cease to fill with tears. I can feel a slight fissure in my heart as I wrestle with my self-control. There is no black and white in this. Safa is not a traitor and the DMC isn't evil. There are just shades of gray. I must remain somewhere in between and not end up like those Sentinels I used to see bullying kids in Prineville just because they were on some power trip. The DMC is serving the greater good, I know this, but obviously innocents like Safa can get caught up in a reluctance to deviate from the rulebook they so closely follow. If I don't keep my perspective, then I could become just like that man who broke my friend's mouth while voices around me cheered him on. A coal of anger forms in the pit of my stomach, as I picture her face and hear their jeers. I leave it there to smolder.

I eventually get up and make my way to the communal shower. It is an open stall with twelve showerheads and multiple drains. I'm thankful that it's late morning and the rest of the recruits are elsewhere. I've never gotten undressed in front of others before and cringe at the thought of future showers with people I don't know. I spend my two minutes of shower time just standing under the spray of water.

I have never actually had a shower before. We were unable to afford to buy our full meal rations with our credits most days, wasting them on water we didn't need was not an option. At home, washing consists of a shallow tub and a sponge. Of course being a Tuesday, even that would be impossible today. It's strange to be standing here under this stream of water while the rest of the people in my town are dry.

I stand under the showerhead and let my tears of anger and grief over Safa mix with the water that streams down my face. I am still standing there five minutes after the water shuts off. I know that I need to accept my fate but it is hard for me to swallow my resentment and face my predicament. Everything here is so foreign, even the other recruits from my town. While I've socialized with them during the initial recruitment process, they are in a whole other caste, one that I was never truly permitted to be a part of. My body is nearly dry by the time I am able to shut my feelings away and leave the shower stall.

The training center is different than I had imagined: large, concrete, and sterile. There are multiple buildings, each identified by a letter, which make up the whole complex along with numerous training areas that are fenced. The entire compound spans acres and is heavily guarded by not only people but also a slew of cameras. The dormitory building is a long, single-story structure dotted with windows that have metal mesh embedded in the glass. I have never been in a building this new before arriving.

As a new recruit, I am not permitted any contact with my family or friends for a period of time. I am sure that it is their way of fully integrating us until our former life is just that, former. I vaguely miss my parents. It is a rather empty feeling when I think of them, somewhat like loss but without the pang of sadness. The person who I see most often behind closed eyes is Safa. I wonder where she is, if she is okay, if she is alive.

My uniform of lightweight, grey pants and shirt emblazoned with the DMC emblem identify me as a new recruit. There are fifteen of us from Prineville and another two-dozen from surrounding towns. Classes begin promptly at seven thirty in the morning. Unlike the classes I took back home, there are no headphones here which make it that much harder for me to separate myself from the present. The first class of the day revolves around the many facets of the DMC from food production to security measures. The late morning and afternoon aptitude classes are the conduit for whatever position I will hold when training is complete.

Aptitude classes consist of everything from weaponry to communications. It is surreal. I float from class to class and see myself doing everything, but I am not really there. As new recruits, we move as a group from room to room. Somehow I always manage to be the last to enter. Many of the classes begin with a computer-generated test. I suppose this acts as a diagnostic tool of some sort from which the Company can begin to designate each recruit into a specific field. The only test that manages to inspire my attention is one that utilizes a series of images that are flashed on the screen. My task is to use my short-term memory to recall specific details. I find that I am good at this and as a result, the program preselects similar tests with increasing difficulty.

In the refectory and dorm, I rarely speak and make only a few sincere attempts to connect with my fellow recruits. Lina is the only one who seems to tolerate me and I find that I can listen and interject at the right times consistently enough that she thinks I'm genuinely interested. But most of them look at me funny since my outburst on the shuttle. There has been more than one time that I've heard them laugh as I walk by or mutter, *crazy pleb*. I can only assume that Agents Sinclair and Banks have noted this. I imagine I can feel their eyes watch my progress.

From outside myself, I watch as the others form their own little cliques, all of them exuding an air of excitement. I generally sit on the sidelines, physically next to Lina in her little crowd, but still separate. The term drones enters my head frequently as I take in their size, strength and glowing health. Of course I have to admit my own improved physical state since my recruitment. But these kids were born for this and have been working toward this their entire lives while I sit wondering how the hell I got here.

At times I feel the stares of one group of drones from another town, once curious and now becoming more hostile. It's like they sense I am not one of them and I become a typical target. I feel like I'm in high school again when one of them intentionally bumps into me as I collect my dinner ration, knocking my tray to the ground.

"Hey!" I yelp as I watch my food splatter onto the floor.

The boy, blond and sun-bronzed, leans into my ear and sneers, "That food is too good for you, pleb. You should eat off the floor where your kind belongs."

I open my mouth, a nasty comment on my tongue,

when I see Agent Banks strolling by the windows just outside. I snap my mouth shut.

"What? Nothing to say?" He jams his shoulder into me as he heads back to a table full of laughter.

I bend down to clean up the mess when I see a pair of shoes in front of me. "Enora, you've gotta try to fit in or you're never gonna make it through training." I hear Lina say.

What she doesn't understand is that I can't fit in, not really. I'm an outsider, despite the uniform that says I'm one of them.

CHAPTER SIX

As the days go by, I find that I am adept at analyzing imagery data. I have always been able to see the details in the world around me but never before has this skill been one that I have been asked to refine. I do recall being able to generate formulas for determining water consumption based on data back in science class, so I guess the analytical skills has always been there in some form.

The equipment that I am given following computerized aptitude tests is a type of binocular. I catch on quickly to the various settings that range from a traditional view to one that creates a coordinate grid of the landscape. From this grid, I can verbally input specific coordinates of various topographical features to create a holographic map of the landscape. As I work to master this tool, I begin to wonder at its uses. Perhaps I could map and locate untapped water sources. This would be a perfect specialty to be a part of and I put my heart into the training.

As I continue to practice using the equipment, I realize that it almost seems like second nature for me to view my surroundings through the scope and note various landmarks or features. In this, I find some peace. When I look through the scope, the rest of the world fades away until all I am aware of is the landscape. If only I could escape into that terrain and leave this all behind.

Perhaps this is all part of the plan because after I find my niche, I slowly begin to accept my fate. Whatever the ulterior motive of the faceless many that are orchestrating everything and regardless of my own angst, I begin to look forward to my training and my instructors take note. They begin to pull me from specific classes in the training forum and take me out into a separate facility, something that elicits resentment from the other recruits. I admit that it's a relief to leave behind recruits like Mica. He's going to be a Sentinel, and not one of the good ones. He's too much of a jerk to put any compassion or understanding into that role.

One instructor, Rafe, takes particular interest in me and as the days pass it becomes apparent that I am being groomed for a specific position. I guess I should feel some alarm. After all, this is not for me. I am not a drone. But as the days and weeks pass it gets harder to maintain my dissenting attitude for my situation. As if from afar, I feel myself slipping away but something dulls any internal warning and I let it happen.

As a reward for my progress, I am given leave to contact my parents. It is good to make the connection and hear that they are doing well in their new unit. Mom even sounds happy, which is quite remarkable.

"Can you believe that our water credits have increased, Enora? For the first time, we've been able to use our full ration. The whole thing! And it's all because of you, baby."

I smile. "That's great, Mom. You and Dad deserve it."

"Oh sweetie, I'm so proud of you for doing this."

It feels kind of strange to hear her gushing like she is, but I suppose not having to scrimp and go without all the time can be so life-changing that her personality would show the effects. As our phone call continues, I talk about small things and listen to them fill me in on this and that, but what I really want to ask is if they have heard anything about Safa. But I can't voice this. Most likely this call is being monitored and I won't take the risk. So my questions sit there inside my head, unanswered and inescapable.

When Rafe comes to the refectory after morning meal a few weeks later and pulls me for a special assignment, I welcome it, feeling pride. As I follow him, I can sense the stares burning in the back of my skull and I allow myself a small, smug smile. I'm sure that it's noted but my own internal high at being singled out makes me feel invincible.

I follow Rafe into the quad. A jeep waits in the lot just outside the main building. "Hop in, Enora, I'm taking you out into the field to see what you can do," Rafe tells me in his deep voice.

I nod. I rarely speak since coming here, even to him. I climb into the jeep, with its electric hum. Rafe drives us out of the training center. We stop at the checkpoint, are scanned and then head through the barbed wire fence and on to the surrounding mountainside. Upon leaving the compound, I feel a weight lifted and take a deep breath of what I deem freedom.

After traveling for what must be an hour, Rafe pulls off the main stretch and we head up a rutted, dirt road to a shrub covered area of the mountain that overlooks a town, one I have never seen before as it is located miles from the training compound. Rafe pulls the jeep to a stop behind some scraggly bushes, at an angle that blocks the view of the vehicle from the other side of the mountain. He jumps out of the jeep. I do the same and then join him as he crouches along the cliff perusing the town below.

It looks so much like Prineville. There are worn buildings from better days dotting the streets, modular housing in organized sections, barbed wire fences bordering the perimeter. I feel a pang of loss as I view it, so much like home and yet a world away. Rafe's voice breaks through my reverie.

"Grab the scope out of the back of the jeep. We're going to see what you can do."

I walk over to the jeep and lift a corner of the tarp covering the back. Pulling out the scope, I begin to wonder just what it is that we are going to be doing today. I have a vague sense that something is wrong and yet no real basis for any unease.

"I want you to set it up under cover of those bushes over there," Rafe says as he points to my right. I have done this many times. The scope has a tripod that is easily extended to any height. I walk over to the bush and pull out the equipment, efficient in my movements, as this has become second nature to me from training. Once the scope is set up, I turn to Rafe. "All set."

He looks at me and then strides over to check the scope. I half smile, there is nothing he will need to adjust. I know what I am doing, and in this, I take some satisfaction. Rafe turns to me, gestures, and then launches into the exercise that he wants me to perform.

"Enora, as you know you have shown great aptitude in using the scope and it has not gone unnoticed by myself or other instructors. We are out here today to see if you can put those skills into action." He pauses and I nod for him to continue.

"The town below us is Clearcreek. You are to locate these following structures."

He hands me grainy satellite images of what look like common facilities you'd see in any town. However, there are a few that I find unusual, as they are more like residences or something of that ilk.

"You have ten minutes."

My eyes bug. Shit! Only ten minutes? I have never

seen this town before and while I know I'm pretty good, this seems unfair. Clearly, I don't say anything aloud, what would be the point? Instead, I ask, "Where is the access point?" All imagery data that I produce using the scope begins with a point of origin. It is like the opening move in a chess game.

Rafe explains that the point of origin is the gully on the eastern perimeter of the border. And that's it. No more information is forthcoming. I decide to start at the town square and work my way out, as most important facilities are usual centrally located. It is the other, less important, structures that make me more nervous under the time constraint. Once I pinpoint each structure I will have to input the data into the scope and then indicate multiple paths from the point of origin to the coordinates of the buildings.

I have done similar tasks at the training center with partially hidden objects set in locations of varying difficulty. I have sharp eyes and the scope allows me to input the location of the object and then map paths through obstacles to that object. Once I have entered the coordinates, the scope generates a three-dimensional map that shows each path that I have identified leading to the object.

But being an actual town adds a layer of realism to the exercise, an element that is absent in the confined training yards. My only consolation is that my position on the mountainside provides an excellent vantage point and the streets are much easier for me to navigate with the scope than some of the maze-like training situations that I have been given prior to today.

I take a deep breath, adjust the scope, and say, "I'm ready."

I lean into the viewfinder and begin scanning the buildings. No more than a few seconds pass when I hear a siren and see people flooding the streets. Ah, so this was the real test. Could I perform the task with a sea of people as an added diversion? I block out all sound and focus. The gully is just outside the border and is easy to locate. I note it with the scope as the base from which my paths will extend. I scan the streets, making calculations that would make the most efficient paths before narrowing in on targets, many of which are indeed located in the center of the town.

An added element of pathfinding is identifying minimally inhabited routes, a task that is becoming increasingly difficult, as the entire populace seems to be emerging at once. From the start, I am forced to delete three of my paths as I note high numbers of people infiltrating the selected channels. It is frustrating, as it almost seems intentional that clusters of humanity are suddenly heading down a route I have found. I begin to wonder if this particular test is one that is rigged to fail in order to see how I handle being unable to complete it. I grit my teeth and shake off the worry, determined to work faster, to get ahead of the swarming masses.

I quickly adjust the scope to get a closer look at each structure and mark two paths to each of the buildings with the mapping system in my unit. The civic center proves more difficult and I don't spot it until I am in the final couple of minutes of my time. I then have to find the last two, the unusual targets. Sweat beads on my forehead as I begin to panic when I can't locate one of the residences. Finally, I spot it and then branch out from that point to identify the last objective. After I mark the final structure and its coordinating paths, I let out a huge breath. In the aftermath, I feel my pulse racing with adrenaline. Layers of sweat have plastered my hair to my head and my hands have a slight tremor as the stress of the training exercise takes full effect. I fight to return my breathing to normal and then turn to Rafe who is looking down at me with a small smile.

"Congratulations, Enora, you have been requisitioned to be a Pathfinder."

I don't think to wonder why we pack up and leave our vantage point so quickly.

CHAPTER SEVEN

The next day I begin to work with Rafe in a special topographical imagery unit in the training center. He explains that my position is part of a larger intelligence unit and that my focus will be to create digital information based on ground observations that can be analyzed and used for various purposes in the intelligence community. It is intensive training through which I learn to use technology I never knew existed.

My assumption is that the technology can be used to locate water resources and map areas that would have the best access to them. But in truth, I'm not sure what all this is for. Rafe is of little help when it comes to insight as he just tells me each assignment is different and the technology has many uses.

It doesn't take long before I find myself becoming more immersed in this place than I want to acknowledge.

And as the days pass, as much as I hate to admit it, I find that I look forward to the specialized training. I have a place here, a purpose. No longer do I feel like I am floating in a sea of hostiles with no buoy to support me when I struggle. I am someone now. I have become a Pathfinder.

There are two other recruits who have been assigned to my training. Lina is one of them and this gives me a sense of comfort, as she's familiar. But I don't care for the other recruit. His name is Nero. I liken him to the worst of the drones in my high school, always ready to target someone who doesn't quite fit in. In this case, that's me. Each day, as we walk to and from our training, he interjects subtle insults and exclusions. It's pretty typical for him to do things like step right in front of me, effectively blocking my path, like I'm too beneath him to walk side by side. Or he refers to me as *pleb*, though I know he is aware of my name. Of course, I've heard this term all my life so it doesn't faze me. He's a drone. What else should I expect?

Lina is pretty good though. Sometimes she chimes in and tells Nero to cut it out. She'll often give me a quick wink after such an instance and I can't help but smile back at her. It's good to have a friend. Sometimes I can't help the thought that she could end up being a better friend than Safa. Such thoughts make me feel queasy and panicky. Is this place changing me more than I realize?

Unfortunately, I still encounter the rest of the drones in the dorm and at every meal. Meal times are some of the worst, followed closely by shower rotations. I hear kids, like Mica and Nero, make comments about how it must be nice to get out of the gutter and eat real food. This type of remark is often followed up by suggestions that I eat their scraps too since I likely won't last too long here. I ignore them until I'm shoved or tripped. When that happens, I either fall on my face or slosh my food all over my uniform.

Shower rotations are a close second in terms of discomfort. Most of the girls just ignore me, but there are handfuls that seem to relish the opportunity to corner me.

"Oh my God. Can you believe they make us share a shower with a pleb?" My eyes are closed as shampoo runs down my face, but I know the voice and hold in my sigh of irritation as Teegan, a drone from another town, goes on. "Hey, Enora. Why don't you suck down some of that water? Maybe it'll fill out that scrawny body and give you some actual boobs."

I can hear snickering from a few girls, but I ignore it. There's no point in saying anything. It's like I have some contagious disease and they never let me forget it. Lina doesn't help much in these situations and I guess I can't blame her. She's probably trying to fit in too and doesn't want to end up a target like me.

And as expected, my transfer to a special program generates more antagonism and I find myself withdrawing further to the perimeter of these antagonistic groups in the hopes of becoming invisible. For the most part I am successful. But Nero doesn't let me forget that I am not truly welcome in any capacity.

"You need to stand up for yourself, Enora." Lina says after one particularly nasty incident when Nero suggested I should end up like my pleb friend he heard was arrested.

I know Lina is trying to be helpful, but she has no idea what its like for me. She only watches from the outside, never feeling what it's like from the inside. But I play along, pretending she's giving me sage advice. "Yeah, I know you're right. I'm just not sure what to say or do. I'm not used to taking a stand."

She looks at me with a patronizing expression. "Obviously you need to say something. Tell him to piss off or something?"

"And have him punch me?" This is a very real possibility in my mind.

"If that's what it takes." There isn't any true understanding in her advice. I get the feeling that she just doesn't want to associate with someone who looks weak. "Look, you have two choices here. Either you continue to let him walk all over you or you stand up to him."

I want to tell off Nero. There are so many comments that I want to let fly, but I always reign it in, too scared to voice them and face the consequences. Maybe Lina is right and I should face up to him. "Okay. I'll try."

"Good."

Being a Pathfinder is not something that I would have envisioned for myself even if I had known of the position. Topography, cartography, geospatial, these terms were not in my vocabulary when I went through school. And yet, when I put my eye to the scope I see landmarks to map with varied routes to each as though I am visualizing a three-dimensional platform. It is an innocuous task that I feel a certain safety and confidence in doing.

In my second week of specialized training another recruit, Drake, is placed in the Pathfinder unit. I had seen him in the dorm, obviously, but never taken any particular notice until now. It surprises me when I feel the stirrings of attraction. He's undeniably handsome, tall and muscular with dark hair and blue eyes. I suddenly feel very awkward. This is a completely foreign feeling for me. The only person I ever felt attracted to was Bram, and I never acted on those impulses. I will have to work to suppress the fluttery feeling that seems to center in my chest when Drake talks to me.

Rafe makes it clear that Drake and I will be working together throughout the remainder of the training, as our skill sets are comparable. Drake is from a small town called Silver Falls. He tells me that most of the people in his town work in underground uranium mines. I'm slightly appalled by this idea. I can't imagine having to work underground. The darkness and confined space would give me the creeps.

Rafe takes to pairing us up for various Pathfinder exercises. I find that while Drake's ability is good, he doesn't have my instincts and this pacifies me somewhat. For whatever reason, I want to exceed him. I try not to analyze this, as I likely won't like what I see. I just accept that this is what I will be doing and I may as well be the best at it.

After one exercise during which I received high praise from Rafe, Drake catches up to Lina and me on our way back to the recruit center for dinner. "Hey, Enora, wait up."

I like the sound of his voice, deep and mellow. "Hi Drake." He smiles at me and I feel my heart go *pitter-pat*, it's embarrassing. Lina looks at me as though trying to figure out why Drake would talk to me and not her. When it's clear that Drake isn't giving Lina any more than a cursory nod in recognition, she rolls her eyes and picks up her pace. Great. That's probably going to come back to bite me.

Drake matches his gait to mine and asks, "So, how are you liking our training? Sure seems like you've got me beat."

I look in his face but see only openness, no rivalry. "I like it, to be honest."

He chuckles. "Well, I can see why. You're a natural."

It feels good to get the compliment. "What about you? I'd say you've got a knack for it yourself."

"Ha. I guess I'm okay."

Our conversation drifts to the mundane and we soon arrive for dinner and part ways. I watch as he heads to a table of kids that seem okay. At least I don't recognize any faces as those belonging to my most frequent tormenters. There is some relief in this. At least Drake isn't like the worst of them.

The next phase of the training takes Drake and I to a remote location of the compound accessible only by vehicle. We exit the jeep, hopping onto the cracked ground baking under the sun and I get my first look at our newest training area. From my vantage point on the ground it appears to be a large, roofless, rectangular structure that extends hundreds of yards in either direction. But upon climbing a ladder to an observation deck, I see that it's a complicated maze.

Our task begins easily enough as we find our way through a network of color-coded targets without encountering any dead ends. I begin to feel my confidence growing as I consistently complete my part of the task within a short time span. I can hear Drake's whoops when he is successful and I can't help grinning.

And then the rigor of the training suddenly reaches new heights as moving objects begin to rise up from previously unnoticed seams in the floor. We now have to avoid these through constant communication while trying to reach the targets.

"Go left. Right. Stop. Okay go." Drake's rapid-fire instructions are jarring as I work from my vantage point.

Next, it's my turn as I see an obstacle enter his section

of the maze-like structure. "Three feet then right. Forward two feet."

And so it goes until we eventually complete the task. In my earpiece, I hear him expel a loud breath. "Damn that was hard."

"Yeah, but we did it." I look across the maze at him in his watchtower and smile.

"We're a good team, Enora."

The compliment sinks into me and I feel my chest swell just a little. "I think so too."

And so the days go by, and as they do I appreciate Drake's quiet companionship and abilities more and more. He has yet to push me for information about myself, though I'm sure he's heard plenty of rumors. I've shared a few things, but I'm reluctant to say too much. Maybe I'm too suspicious, but I keep thinking about Safa. She trusted someone and that person could've turned her in. I don't want to open myself up to such a risk by talking about the crime my friend is accused of. I like Drake, I just don't know how much I trust him. Only time will tell, I suppose.

I am leaving our unit alone one evening, Lina having ditched me days ago, when I hear Drake call out to me, "Hey, Enora, wait up."

I stop midstride. I watch him jog over. He's so strong. You can see the strength in every line of his body.

When he reaches my side he surprises me by asking, "Want to join me in the refectory for dinner?"

I feel my mouth drop open. Wow, didn't expect him to

ask to sit with me. I mean we often walk together at the end of the day but sitting in a room full of watching eyes is new and unexpected. "Um...oh...okay."

As we walk, I steal glances at Drake from the corner of my eye. What's his agenda? Should I be suspicious or have I become totally paranoid?

I can't help but note how he walks with such confidence. Head held high, eyes forward, not looking down at his feet as I so often do. He's so confident. I find myself wishing I were that self-assured.

We reach the dorm and he surprises me by touching my arm and saying, "See you at dinner."

Then he jogs off to his small clique of friends. I stand there for a moment watching him. Then open the door to the dorm and head to my bunk for some down time. There is a thirty-minute free period during which I always like to write in my journal. It is my way of keeping my balance in a situation that could tip my perceptions toward a side I am careful to avoid.

The dinner hour arrives and suddenly I am nervous. Since coming to the training center, I have gone out of my way to keep a low profile, especially at meals. I am now facing the idea of sitting with Drake and potentially his group of friends. My heart starts to pound and I feel an unwelcome sense of panic building inside me. I try to tamp it down as I head for the refectory. I place my arm in the scanner, pick up my meal, and stand there feeling awkward and looking stupid. This only serves to increase the pounding of my already racing heart. I am so anxious that when I hear Drake's voice in my ear I nearly drop my tray.

He chuckles. "Did I scare you?" His eyes are dancing with amusement. I manage a glare. "Come on, let's sit by the window."

I assume we are heading to his usual table, but to my surprise he leads me away from his comrades to an unoccupied table with a view of the quad. As we weave our way through the hall, I feel the looks. He must sense them too, but while I feel myself shrinking into my shell like a turtle, Drake remains as self-possessed as ever. Now that I think about it, his confidence is rather annoying. I make a face and sit across from him.

Drake notices my reaction. "Don't worry about them, Enora. They're just a bunch of spoilt kids. You're so much better than they are."

"Yeah, right." I mutter.

He shakes his head. "I'm serious. You've got talent none of them will ever have. Most of them are gonna end up as guards, patrolling stockyards that stink of cow shit. Don't let them get to you, okay?"

"I'll try."

We make it to a table and I sit down, feeling awkward. I have never been a conversation starter. It's just not my thing. I prefer to listen and chime in when I feel I can actually contribute to the dialogue. So it is extremely awkward for me to be sitting with him under this air of expectancy. I should have known Mr. Confidence would break the silence first.

"So, what do you think of Rafe?"

It's a good question, neutral ground, and something he seems to know I'll not hesitate to volunteer information about.

"He's been good to me. He certainly knows what topographical imagery is all about. I like him, though he can be pretty demanding."

"That's an understatement," Drake volunteers. "But I agree, he's a good guy and will train us well. I'm glad he's in charge of our unit."

And then I ask, "Do you ever wish you were placed in another unit, with someone else?"

I want to suck the words back into my mouth the moment they are spoken, embarrassed. Instead all I can do is bite my lip and look away, suddenly unsure. But Drake surprises me.

"No."

That's it. Just no. But it's enough because when I swing my eyes back to him I can see more than that simple word. It seems I have a real friend, with a drone of all people. Who would've thought? I smile and dig into my meal.

I feel like this is a turning point. While I don't trust Drake completely, I'm not as guarded as I was before. He senses it too and the next day waits for me just outside the dorm so that we can walk together to our unit. I still feel eyes on me as I walk through the quad, and maybe I'm being naïve, but they don't feel as threatening as before. I decide to be thankful for little things. I throw myself into my training while exploring new territory. I begin to relax and feel that I have made my peace with my lot in life. I should have known it wouldn't last.

CHAPTER EIGHT

I don't plan on eavesdropping. I just heard my name so I duck behind a corner without even thinking about it. Leaving seems silly when I can just listen for a bit and find out what is being said. I lean my head as close to the edge of the wall as possible to catch the conversation.

I hear Rafe's voice. "She's got great instincts and her mapping skills are excellent."

"That's good to hear. I had wondered about her placement, after the incident in her hometown." The voice is a man's and sounds recognizable but I resist the urge to peek and potentially give myself away.

"I can see why you were concerned but I assure you that she has put all of her effort into this role. I see great potential." A smile spreads across my face when I hear Rafe say this. I've never been a standout kid who was noticed for anything exceptional and now my skills are being recognized. My head swells with pride, just a little.

That familiar voice interjects again. "When do you think she'll be ready to join her counterpart? I've tentatively selected someone for her and he's ready to get started immediately."

There is a brief pause. "I would say less than a week. I want to introduce her to some software programming, as I believe she'll be quite adept. I think it would benefit her work with you to understand various network applications, especially if she could eventually be accessing backdoors into systems or performing overrides to obtain information."

I imagine the other man's head nodding and wish I could see this whole interaction. "Good."

"I have to tell you, her work in Clearcreek surpassed my expectations. I'm sure you've received a briefing, but thought you should know that her trajectories were spot on and allowed the Sweeper to move in completely undetected." Rafe's compliment is confusing to me. While I know that I had plotted the most efficient routes, I'm not sure what he means by a Sweeper following my paths. I never saw anyone move in after I had finished the task.

"Excellent. That was a sensitive situation that could've turned ugly if our actions had been discovered."

"I agree. But all targets were eliminated and staged without incident and I feel that a large part of the success rests in Enora's innate ability." Rafe's voice is dripping with pride while my mind begins to piece together what he's saying.

"She is an asset to the program. You will hear from me shortly with her assignment." I can hear their bodies shift as the man adds, "Keep up the good work."

Their footsteps eventually recede and I find myself sliding to the floor. A Sweeper came in after me? Of course, I know what a Sweeper is. You don't go through any training here without an overview of the various roles we could be assigned to. Sweepers are just what their name implies. They come in and clean up the mess. But I was supposed to be using my mapping skills to search for resources. Not this. This was just a test, a way to see how advanced my abilities have become.

A thought floats through my brain that my assumptions were just that, ideas with no real substance. Regardless, this is what I had been prepared to do. Finding water in our dry world was a perfect way for me to put my skills to use. I never faced the other possibilities.

Why else would they ask you to map a town, Enora? It feels like betrayal but if it is, it's my own betrayal. I'm the one who convinced myself it would be this harmless thing. No one did that for me.

Oh God. A Sweeper came in after me. Rafe said he eliminated targets. I tell myself that I didn't know, that it isn't my fault, but that's not really true. I knew something was off but had ignored my instincts. My role isn't generating digital intelligence data for the good of the people.

It's creating a way to snuff out the undesirable elements in the most efficient way possible, with no witnesses, and no recourse.

I have become a weapon.

The knowledge shakes me as nothing ever has. It wasn't supposed to be like this. I feel so *stupid*! I've thrown myself into the training. In fact, now that I look at myself, I mean really look, where am I? Where is that girl whose utopia consisted of quiet camaraderie and some shade to rest under? It feels as though parts of me have been slowly erased, no dramatic shift, simply a careful process through which I morphed into a weapon, their weapon. When I look at myself in the mirror, will I see Enora? Or will I see a drone?

I get up from my hidden spot and head for the dorm, hoping to avoid anyone on my way. Once there, I take a quick glance to make sure I'm alone before running to the comfort of my bed. I sit on my bunk, wishing I had never overheard Rafe. My stomach roils with the knowledge of what I was a part of. This is not what the DMC is supposed to represent. They are here to protect us, not do harm. Only those people who are traitors should be targets.

I calm myself and take a few deep breaths. I need to think this over. What if those people the Sweeper eliminated were water traitors? Would this punishment be appropriate? I feel myself trying to rationalize the consequences when Safa's face enters my mind.

Could I map a route to kill her? No. There is nothing she could do that would convince me to just take her life.

What if those people in Clearcreek were just like Safa? No, no they were not like Safa. Safa was a kid and this wouldn't happen to a kid. She's probably back at home right now, bruised and battered but wiser. The people in Clearcreek must have been a part of a rebel faction or something. Perhaps they were water traitors on such a large scale that the whole town has been suffering for a long time.

I play this scenario over in my head. The DMC wouldn't do this to Safa. These people were true traitors. It has to be that.

DRAKE IS WAITING FOR ME OUTSIDE THE REFECTORY for evening meal.

I must still look like a wreck because he asks, "Hey, you feeling okay?"

He must not know. I imagine the truth is stamped across my face. I feel like I must look different...murderer. It may have been for the right reasons but stain of guilt is there. I helped take lives. They may have been rebels, but they were also human beings. I feel like it's changed me.

But I lie and tell him, "Yeah, I was feeling queasy earlier but I'm fine now."

I avert my eyes hoping that he won't see the fib in them. When I don't hear a reply I peek at him and find his brows knit in a frown. He knows, he sees it. But then he looks up, shakes it off, and pulls me along through the doors.

I can feel myself withdrawing from him as we sit at what has become our usual table by the window. He's unobtrusive, perhaps sensing my mood, and doesn't push me for conversation. It is this quiet acceptance that is nearly my undoing. I feel like I need to purge myself. Get the venom out, but I force myself to rein it in by biting the inside of my cheek.

He finally breaks the silence. "I heard Rafe talking about you this morning."

My eyes spring to his in alarm. Oh God, does he know? Will he look at me differently now?

"Yeah, he was singing your praises all right. You know, about how you set a new personal best yesterday."

I give a jerky nod as he pauses. "Thanks a lot, by the way. I mean you know I'm never going to be able to top that, right? You're making me look bad," he says with a smile.

I sit there for a moment, waiting for the proverbial 'other shoe' to drop, but it doesn't. That's all he says.

"Is that all Rafe said?" I ask, hoping he'll say yes but dreading that he'll say no.

"What? Those praises aren't good enough for you?" His eyes are twinkling and a grin is playing around the corners of his mouth. "Well, Miss Ego, unfortunately, yeah, that's all that he said. Never said a word about me."

He tries to look glum, but it's ruined by the chuckle under his breath.

I pull myself together, plastering a phony condescending look on my face and say, "I guess I could give you some pointers."

He guffaws, shakes his head, and plows through his food. I force myself to put on a mask that shields my inner battle and struggle through the meal, adding small bits of conversation to avoid appearing indifferent while also avoiding suspicion. It's not easy but sadly I am getting better at the deception. Soon, it'll be second nature and I will find myself able to hide everything.

I toss and turn in my bunk that night, replaying the scene from Clearcreek over and over in my head. The guilt is crushing. I feel as though there is a boulder sitting on my chest and no matter how I shift my body, there is no relief. Dawn is approaching and I don't know what to do. I can't tell Drake. I mean, maybe he'd turn me in for being a traitor to the Company. A dark image creeps into my mind, Drake, crouched with a Sweeper, hunting for targets. Does he know why we're being trained? I want to deny it, but I fear that he does. And beneath that fear, a dread that he embraces it. I force my mind to go back to those shades of gray. I need to do my part for the DMC, but I also need to hold onto my humanity. I fear that the moment I see these traitors as less than human, is when I lose myself entirely.

By the time the sun filters through the windows, I have made the only decision I can regarding Drake. I will pretend that I heard nothing of Rafe's conversation and will bury my anxiety under a façade of dedication to my training. I will watch and wait. It's my only choice.

Do not search for me
Nor see what I am
For when you find me
When you look
You will ***see*** *me*
Tarnished, tainted
Sick with the knowledge
Of what I have become
Of what you are

CHAPTER NINE

I am pulled from training and taken to a nondescript office on the second story of the main building. It looks different here, soft, homey. There is carpet on the floor. I have only seen carpet once when my class had gone on a tour of the Prineville Civic Center. This carpet looks much nicer, newer. I can't stop myself from leaning down and stroking the soft tufts that cover the floor. I try to distract myself in the sensation. But I'm only partly successful.

Inside, questions are popping around my head. What are they going to ask me? Did they find out I was spying on their conversation? Did Drake tell them I didn't seem quite right? With each question, my nerves make me feel more rattled.

The office door opens so quietly, that I am completely oblivious. I am actually sinking my hand into the plush texture of the carpeting, while talking to myself in my head, when I hear a throat clear and look up into a pair of eyes that I had never thought to see again.

My heart actually stops and then stutters before regaining its normal rhythm as I look into Bram's face. "Ms. Byrnes," he says formally. Not his voice, I can't help thinking. I realize that it was him I heard speaking to Rafe. No wonder it sounded so familiar, different, older, but familiar. "Please have a seat."

Bram indicates one of the large, leather chairs opposite a desk and I awkwardly rise, flustered, embarrassed, and frightened, before lowering myself onto the cool cushion.

"I understand that your Pathfinder training is going exceptionally well," he says while thumbing through a thick folder of information that must undoubtedly be about me. He looks up when I offer no response. "You must be surprised to see me."

I find my voice and say, "It's been over two years, Bram. Have you been here the whole time?"

He leans back in his chair, steeples his fingers and says, "Not the whole time, but I requested that I be reassigned to this center." It's an odd statement and one that he doesn't elaborate on. Instead, he shifts in the chair and launches into the reason for requesting my presence.

"It has come to the attention of the head trainer that you have exceeded expectations and are ready to be placed with a counterpart to finalize your training so that you can go into the field full time."

My heart breaks a little when he says this. It feels like betrayal. Has he forgotten all of our plans, our talks of escaping all of this and living free? And then I realize that, like me, he has been erased. And while I am fighting to preserve a part of my humanity, he has let go of his. To him, it is all black and white. My shoulders drop and I nod my understanding.

"You will begin working with a Sweeper tomorrow morning. He has been in the program for some time and will be your counterpart as you enter the field. He will fully explain your role in a briefing first thing in the morning. It is important that you put as much effort into this new phase of your training as you have up to this point." He pauses, flips to a form near the front of the folder and scans the document.

Looking up he says, "Your counterpart will be Sergeant Ethan Springer. He will train you in how to work as a unit unto yourselves and will report directly to me." I realize that, in essence, Bram has become the facilitator of my new role. Tears prick my eyes, but I stubbornly blink them back, grit my teeth and listen to him finish.

"As a unit, you and Springer will eventually enter the field for specific operations. As your supervisor, I will be intricately involved throughout this process." He pauses briefly before saying, "I realize that this is a lot to take in, especially in light of our past. Do you have any questions that I can address?"

I want to scream, yes! How can you do this to me?

You, of all people, know me, the real me. But when I look into Bram's face, I see that he doesn't. He's gone and he doesn't recognize the monster that I am becoming. He doesn't try to stop its mad progression. Instead, he is encouraging its growth.

I square my shoulders, stubbornly refusing to let him see the grief I am feeling, and formally say, "No, sir. I believe I understand the basics of my new role and your expectations."

He raises an eyebrow. "No questions at all? You have no curiosity about your role?"

I look him in the eyes. "I don't feel it is my place to question the assignment you've given to me."

When I finish, something flashes in his eyes, but it is gone before I am able to identify what it is. Then he is standing, extending his hand for me to shake it, and saying, "Welcome to the unit, Ms. Byrnes."

I HAVE NO MEMORY OF WALKING BACK TO THE training area. I do not recall picking up my scope, going through an exercise, nor hearing Drake gloat when he completes the task three full minutes before I do. I am undone.

Drake doesn't continue to razz me about my rather lackluster performance and we pass through the afternoon completing various exercises before the siren blares, marking the end of the day. I return my scope to the locker, taking an unnecessary amount of time to clean and pack it, before heading to the dorm for solitude prior to supper.

Drake is waiting for me at our regular table by the time I've grabbed my meal. I can see that whatever questions my earlier behavior elicited, are going to be verbalized now. As I make my way through the maze of tables, Lina steps in front of me, blocking my path.

"Hey, Lina."

She looks at Drake, then back at me. "Are you sitting with Drake again?"

"Um, yeah."

I watch as her eyes travel over my body in some kind of analysis. "Did he seriously ask you to join him again? I mean, not to be a bitch, but he's hot and you're...well, you're not."

I want to roll my eyes, but manage to keep them still. "I know it's a little weird, but he's cool and we've got a lot in common."

Lina's eyebrows rise in disbelief. "Oh." Then she tosses her head and says, "Well, if he ever wants to join my table, tell him he's got an open invitation."

"Okay. I'll let him know."

She gives me a hard look, and in it, I finally see the jealously that I didn't recognize earlier. "You do that."

She moves aside and I slowly continue onward, but find myself looking back at her as she returns to her table. I see her lean into Nero and whisper something. His head turns toward me and he smirks. I hear him make some comment to his whole table that makes all of them look my way and laugh. I should know better than to trust a drone. Lina has always been one, and nothing will change that.

Drake waits until I'm sitting next to him. "What's going on, Enora?"

"It's nothing. They're just being themselves, picking on the pleb as usual."

I watch as Drake turns his attention to Lina's group and see him frown. I follow his eyes and meet Lina's. She glares at me and I know I've made a mistake, crossed some imaginary line. I sigh and begin to dig into my meal.

Drake mutters something unintelligible, and then says, "Nero is such an asshole."

I couldn't agree more but don't bother adding anything. We sit in comfortable silence for a bit, simply using the time to fill our bellies. But eventually I see his body shift and know the time has come for a more serious conversation.

Drake puts down his fork. "You've been acting kind of strange lately, but it seems like today you're even worse. Why were you called away?"

I want to let it all out. It's like a festering sore that needs lancing. I feel the words bubbling inside me, ready to spill over the surface. I open my mouth, no longer able to stop the tide, and let out a short sob. I try to suck it back in as I furtively look around me to make sure no one is watching us. I sense Drake scoot a bit closer. His nearness calms me and allows me to pull myself together.

When my breath stops catching, I say what I have feared to utter. "I feel trapped. This path I'm on has consequences I never considered and there is no way to step off it and find a new direction. They are taking me away and turning me into something...else. There's nothing I can do to stop it."

Once it's out, I almost regret the words, but in the end, who cares? Isn't it better to just get it out, even if the repercussions are severe?

He lets out a whoosh of air. "I wasn't sure if I could trust you. I've been watching you for weeks, but until now, I thought you were one of them."

Drake's announcement stuns me. He smiles. "Yeah, I fooled ya didn't I?"

I must look shocked. "Oh my God, I have wasted time, wanting to tell you, but too scared to do it. I thought you were a drone."

"Drone? What the hell is a drone?"

I smile, a little embarrassed at having to explain. "Well, you see....hm. I don't want to offend you or anything but you're kind of a perfect example of one."

"That doesn't sound very flattering, Enora."

I wrinkle my nose. "It's not. Okay. Look around the room and tell me what you notice about all of the people here."

I watch as Drake takes in a panoramic view. "They're all real fit."

"Yep. What else?"

He looks the room over again. "I'm into girls and all, just to be clear, but I'd say that everyone here is really good looking."

His head is slightly tilted, allowing his eyes to look up at me when he says this last part. I laugh. "Are you implying that I'm ugly?"

"No! That's not what I meant!" He seems sincerely upset.

I bat my hand at him. "Don't worry about it. I've seen myself in the mirror and I know I don't look like the rest of these kids. Everyone in this room, myself excluded and you included, is tall, muscular and damn good looking. In other words, drones."

Drake leans back in his chair and rolls his eyes. "Oh my God. I'm a drone."

"You sure are. And I bet your parents, and the parents of every other kid in this room, are Sentinels or have some higher-ranking position."

"Crap. Is that the other drone-characteristic?"

"Indeed it is and from your reaction, I'm betting I'm right." I smirk at him.

He snorts. "Fine. I'm a drone. What's that make you?"

"As if you didn't already know, I'm a pleb. My folks work at the mill outside of town. How I managed to get here is becoming one of the great mysteries of the world." I can't keep a straight face after I say this and spend a couple of minutes laughing with him. It feels good to laugh.

After our mirth has died down, Drake goes on to tell me how his father works at his town's DMC headquarters and that, as a result, it is expected that he and his siblings will follow suit in high-ranking positions. There was never an option for him with regard to recruitment and he has lived his life knowing it. It feels good to talk, to really talk, and have someone listen and understand. I realize that I have craved this, been starved for a friendly ear. Lina never asked me about my interests or anything, really. I was just some lost soul following in her shadow. Drake is different. He seems to feel the same. Before we walk to our dorm rooms, we agree to meet after curfew. It's a risk, but Drake assures me that he knows a place we can hide in.

It must be close to midnight when I deem it safe to venture out of my bunk to meet Drake. I am eager to see him. It is as though by spilling my secrets I have opened a new door. I walk silently through the rows of bunks, my heart stopping each time I hear a rustle or soft snore. I let out a relieved breath when I enter the dimly lit hallway that connects the two wings of the dormitory. Drake's sleeping quarters are at the opposite end of the building, in the men's section. My bare feet pad softly along the cool tiles as I make my way down the hallway and around a corner. There are no cameras in the dorms so being spotted by an all-seeing eye is one less thing to worry about.

I find Drake at our designated meeting spot, an alcove between our sections of the building. He takes my hand and pulls me into a supply closet. We forgo the light, using the hallway illumination instead, in the hope that we will not be found. I find a bucket and silently flip it over to use as chair. Drake does the same and we sit facing each other in the cramped space, feeling awkward and giddy.

I break the stillness first, unable to control my need to tell him what I overheard from Rafe. I keep my voice low. "You know how you said that Rafe was talking about me?"

"Yeah."

"Well, I thought you were going to tell me about what I overheard."

"What'd you hear?"

I take a breath. "My test at Clearcreek was more than a test. Apparently there was a Sweeper who came in after I had completed my task." There is no need to explain what this means as we have a common understanding of the role.

"I see. And you feel this makes you a part of it?"

"Of course it does!" I take a moment to temper my voice. "I'm the one who mapped the routes that were used to eliminate whomever was targeted. I'm a killer. That blood is on my hands, the same as it would be if I was there pulling a trigger."

Drake is silent for a few minutes and I fiddle with my sleeping gown in worry as I wait. "Have you considered that these people were traitors?"

"Yes. I know they are, but they are still people."

He nods. "And that's something we need to always remember. I get the guilt you're feeling, but what is it you thought you were preparing for?"

I look away, my eyes roving the shelves of supplies. "I lied to myself, Drake. I told myself that this role was designed to help people. That maybe I'd map areas of water resources or something."

"It might be that, Enora."

"Oh sure."

"What? You don't think they're going to have us do different things? I'm banking on it. I mean, do you think I want to be just putting down rebel forces all the time? There's gotta be more to it than that."

"I hope you're right. I almost wish we could just escape, you know?" This is what Bram and I always dreamed and now that dream is dead. Perhaps I can live it with Drake.

He sighs. It's a mournful sound and before he utters a word I know what he will say. "How, Enora? You've mapped every boulder and crevice as far as the scope will let you. Where would we go? There is nothing out there but dust and death."

He's right. I know he's right, but how can I play along when inside I'm feeling like I'm splitting apart?

"Listen to me." He raises my chin so that I am looking into his eyes. "You need to do this. There is no other choice. There never was a choice, not for us. You need to play the part. Do you understand? If you don't...."

He swallows and looks away. Drake doesn't need to finish the thought. There is only one consequence for traitors within the Company.

We huddle next to each other for a while longer until I am unable to stifle a yawn and Drake says, "Come on. We better try to get some sleep."

I walk down the hall, darting into a recessed area when someone from my dorm heads into the bathroom. I finally make it to my bed, lie down, and fall into a deep sleep the moment my head hits the pillow.

I have awful dreams. I watch myself as if from outside my body. I am a Pathfinder, marking routes to facilities in my own town, and watch later as friends, even my family, are taken out by the Sweeper working with me, and yet I keep marking paths to other locations, unfazed by the ugly truth of what I am doing. No conscience, no hesitation. Enora is gone and in her place is a killer.

I wake up with a scream building in my throat and feel my body being roughly shaken. I yelp as I see Lina's face just inches from mine.

"You're moaning in your sleep and woke me up."

I try to clear my head. "Sorry. I had a nightmare."

"Well maybe if you didn't go traipsing off at all hours, you'd sleep better and not disturb the rest of us." There is coldness in her face as she looks me over and then heads back to her bed across the aisle. I'm vulnerable now. And she knows it.

I close my eyes and concentrate on regulating my heart that has been racing since the moment I awoke. I push aside the threat in Lina's statement, as there is nothing I can do about it anyway. There are other things to consider right now. When I have regained some semblance of control, I open my eyes and stare into the darkness until the dusky pink of dawn shines through the windows. I will meet my Sweeper today.

CHAPTER TEN

Rafe is waiting for me outside the refectory after the morning meal. He indicates that I should follow him and we make our way into the commons. From the corner of my eye I can see Drake lingering in the hallway, watching me. I quickly avert my eyes. As we walk, I begin clenching and unclenching my hands. Lina must have talked. She's such a spiteful bitch and I wish that I could retaliate or stand up to her, but I know I won't. Rafe and I enter the center of the quad and turn toward an unfamiliar building. I'm momentarily distracted by it when I hear him clear his throat.

"I wanted to talk to you about something, Enora."

"Yes, sir?" Did my voice crack?

"There are certain rules that all instructors expect of recruits. One of those is fraternization. If you find yourself entertaining the idea of messing around with a boy, I suggest you either squelch it or find a better hiding spot."

My face feels frozen. He looks over at me, waiting for a response and my cheeks flame. "I apologize. It won't happen again."

"Be sure that it doesn't. Or at the very least, be aware of who might be watching." He winks at me and I feel a whoosh of air leave me.

I try to smile, but I'm sure it looks awkward. "I will. Thank you for...you know...for being understanding."

"You're welcome. Now, let me give a quick rundown before we head inside."

Rafe explains that I will be preparing for fieldwork and will meet my counterpart, Springer. At the entrance to the building, I have to place my arm in a scanner to unlock the door. The additional security is a bit of a surprise but I assume that there must be a reason for it. The door opens and Rafe leads me through a corridor and into section A of the building.

He leads me up a flight of stairs to a large room and indicates a young man who is crouched on the floor assembling a weapon. "That's Sergeant Ethan Springer. Good luck, Enora." And with a gesture of his head, he leaves.

I take a few moments to look Springer over. He is engrossed in his task. He wears a black uniform, not a recruit I say to myself, with some type of vest. I can see that he is quite tall, though he has yet to stand, and that his body exudes wiry strength. He looks to be two or three years older than me, but no more than that. I feel so small and helpless just looking at him. Images of my dream resurface and I can suddenly picture us working side by side, assassins. My stomach clenches at the thought and I feel a chasm of hopeless fear opening inside me.

The sharp click of a gun yanks me back to reality and I watch as Springer places the rifle on the floor and stands. It seems as if he turns in slow motion, his height eclipsing mine. His skin is deeply tanned, browned by the sun after countless hours in the field, which makes his green eyes almost startling in his chiseled face. His thick, black hair is cropped short, unmistakably for efficiency. He looks like a drone, not as breathtakingly handsome as Drake, but good-looking and brawny like the rest of them. As I have been assessing him, he has been assessing me. I am dwarfed by his size and strength. He strides toward me with a loose gait, extending his hand.

"Enora, I'm Springer. I understand that we are going to be working together," he says in a voice that hints at an accent I am not familiar with.

I extend my hand and feel his powerful, calloused fingers encompass mine in a firm shake. I manage to stammer out, "Good morning."

"I've heard great things about you. Rafe has been singing your praises and Commander Williams feels that our abilities will pair nicely." He has a soothing voice, which seems at odds with his large frame.

"Thank you. I hope to live up to the praise."

"I'm sure you will." Springer cracks a smile that gives him a boyishly handsome expression. "Now, let me fill you in on our partnership."

He clasps his arms behind his back and launches into an explanation of our roles. I listen half-heartedly, already understanding the primary reason for our partnership. I will be locating and marking a path to targets with the scope and he will be eliminating them. It is really quite straightforward and awful in its simplicity. After Springer outlines the basics he says, "Now, you do realize that any targets we are assigned have been identified by the DMC as terrorists."

I'm taken aback by his casual reference to killing. While I now understand the potential for this, I haven't come to any comfort level with it. It just seems so brutal. "How do they determine who's a terrorist?"

Springer cocks an eyebrow. "We are not privy to that process, Enora. Our role is very specific."

My expression must give my internal battle away because I see his eyes narrow slightly. "Is this position going to be a problem? Do I need to speak with the Commander?"

Shit. I've really stepped in it this time. Am I crazy? What the hell is wrong with me? "I did not mean to imply that I find fault with the process. I'm sorry. This is all very new and I was up most of the night with nervous energy." While he doesn't look completely convinced, he seems somewhat mollified.

"All right, let's get started."

Springer spends the morning teaching me how to use various communications equipment as well as hand signals that we will be using should our communicators go out. When the midday meal announcement resounds through the building, I am told that I will be having the noon meal here, as all special operatives do. I feel a slight pang as I imagine Drake waiting for me outside the refectory before eventually realizing that I am not coming.

Springer leads me to a large room. We place our arms in the reader and head inside, greeted by a large spread of food. My mouth drops open. I have never seen such a variety of food before. There are three full platters of meat, real meat. One is beef, that special delicacy, and the other two are pork and chicken. Next to these are bowls of potatoes, carrots, cobs of corn, cooked spinach, salad greens, soft rolls, and a large crock of butter. On another table is an assortment of fruit, some I have never tasted like pineapple. With this are plates of desserts of all kinds, from cookies to little pies. It is a feast of shocking proportions and I can't wait to dig in.

I hear Springer chuckle beside me and say, "I think I had that exact reaction the first time I walked into this room."

He explains that all specialists have certain privileges including better food and housing, though the latter will not be available to me until I have proven myself as a Pathfinder. I am handed a warm plate as I eye the mouthwatering dishes, trying to decide where to start. I start with the main table and fill my plate with a sampling of everything, creating a small mountain. There is no way that I will be able to eat all of this, but I was equally unable to stop myself from taking it. Springer leads me to an empty table and we begin our meal. I am about halfway through my lunch, struggling not to moan in gastronomical ecstasy, when the door swings open and Bram walks in.

The partially chewed meat in my mouth suddenly feels like a lump of wet sand as I watch him fill a plate and head directly to my table. I struggle to chew and gulp down some water to get the food down my throat, as Bram pulls out the chair next to me and sits. My eyes shift to my plate, appetite gone.

"Enora, Springer," Bram says by way of a greeting. I bob my head in acknowledgement.

"Commander," Springer replies with a dip of his head.

As I observe how deferential Springer is, I wonder, just how powerful *is* Bram? I quickly assess how long he has been with the DMC and cannot fathom how he could reach such a high rank in so short a time. And then, I begin to think that perhaps I wouldn't want to know the story behind his quick accession. I look at Springer, who seems at ease in his commander's presence.

Bram turns his gaze to me and asks, "How is Enora acclimating to her new position this morning?"

Oh crap, I think to myself. He's going to tell Bram about my question and I'm going to get hell for it. But

Springer surprises me when he replies, "She's smart and has already shown some mastery of the communication devices."

Bram nods. "Very good. Please keep me informed through a daily report."

"Yes, sir."

My plate of food, half eaten, now looks unappetizing. I push it around with my fork as I listen to Bram and Springer discuss more important things than me. When Bram has finished his meal, he rises, wishes us a good afternoon, and leaves. I sense Springer looking at me and turn to him. His brow is creased in questioning and I wait for him to ask what he must be thinking.

"Do you know the Commander?"

I am not sure how to answer. Am I supposed to pretend that I had never seen him until coming here or is it acceptable to admit the truth? I decide that a half-truth would be best.

"He's from my town and was ahead of me in school. I used to see him around, but never knew him well." It isn't until the words have left my mouth that I realize how true they are. Seeing Bram now, I realize that I truly didn't know him.

Springer seems to accept this as truth and concentrates on finishing the remaining food on his plate.

. . .

The afternoon portion of the training brings what I have been dreading. Springer starts by pulling out his weapon. He explains that it is a high-powered rifle with specialized capabilities including synchronization with the scope's mapping system. A small hologram illuminates above the eye piece revealing the paths that I have marked. This allows him to easily follow a path and reach a target with minimal risk.

"It reduces error in the field," he tells me.

He says it so nonchalantly. Error, as in the wrong person gets eliminated. These are people we're talking about, but from the way he says it they may as well be cockroaches.

"Your role is essential in the field, as you will be able to mark multiple paths in the space of a few minutes while I position myself. Without your Pathfinder capabilities, we could lose precious time or the target could evade us altogether. That's why satellites aren't an option and we need you on the ground. There're simply not enough satellites available to get accurate images for so many targets. A Pathfinder monitors the situation in real time." He continues, unfazed by my lack of response. "The majority of the time you will be located in an elevated position, much like you were at Clearcreek, and I will be at the point of origin. You will identify the most efficient route and then communicate your readiness to me."

He has my complete attention now. I think to myself, he knows about Clearcreek?

I can't help asking, "Were you there? At Clearcreek, I mean."

"Certainly," he says, as if I should know this little piece of information. "I was a Sweeper, your Sweeper actually. We had not been formally placed together but I was there as your counterpart. Good job, by the way. Your trajectories were spot on." He's smiling at me when he gives the compliment and I feel a little sick inside. "Once a team has completed an assignment, the Cleaners are provided with location intel and destroy evidence. Each town or city has one or more of these teams which enables a scene to be cleansed before civilians can stumble upon it."

He killed them and then people just came in and cleaned it all up as if nothing happened. Oh my God, I marked the path that he followed to kill them. I start to feel queasy. How did he do it? Were they shot? Did they see him coming? What had they done? Questions keep buzzing around my head. Questions that I can't ask but need to ask. I need to know, but at the same time I don't want to face the truth. I hear Springer's voice in the background, a low hum that I can't concentrate on. I can't do this, I tell myself. I can't kill people.

And then his words start to piece together and I hear him say, "Of course, I can't always use the rifle. There are times when I need to be much more subtle. In those cases, your job is to stay in contact with me and keep an eye on the situation." I watch as he unstraps a large knife from his hip and casually flips it in the air before catching the handle. "At those times, I use this baby. I have to get closer than I like, but I keep it quiet."

My imagination conjures up an awful scenario and the last thing I want is to hear any more of the details of his more creative work. Thankfully, I'm saved from having to listen to specifics as Springer continues. "Ultimately, Enora, my life depends on the choices you make and the efficiency with which you carry those decisions out."

I reflect briefly on what he has said, on the power that is clearly in my hands. I take the opportunity to ask the question that is burning in my brain. "What if I can't do it? I may not be pulling the trigger, but it's me doing the killing just as much as it is you."

Springer nods, a little surprised, but seeming to understand my question. Perhaps he has been anticipating it. Maybe other Pathfinders have asked something similar.

He takes a moment to think, choosing his words carefully. "Enora, I'm not going to lie and tell you that it's easy. This is a difficult job that not only takes certain skill, but a strong will. Our first official assignment may be a challenge for you, but I guarantee that it will become easier. You must remember that these targets are threats to our society. I've seen terrorists blow up a DMC headquarters in the middle of a city. Hundreds were killed, women and children. We're the good guys here, Enora. It's up to us to protect the public. Think of the greater cost of *not* eliminating them."

The greater cost. I think this over. What were those targets in Clearcreek planning that they had to be eliminated? Did they have an opportunity to explain their side? I know I can't ask, but to me this whole thing seems a bit ruthless and unfair.

It's the whole black and white perspective rearing its ugly head again. I keep drifting toward that middle ground, especially when I think of Safa and the consequences of her actions. I want to be one of the 'good guys' like Springer is describing, but I also accept that there are two sides to every story.

But what if they were planning an attack like the one Springer talked about? What if their agenda is simply resistance no matter the cost? What if children died because no one stepped in to stop it? I need time to think this through.

"What if I accidentally track the wrong person? What if someone who's innocent gets killed?"

Springer reaches over and takes my hand. I try to pull away from him, but his grip is too strong. "What are you...?"

"Sssh. Look." He turns my left hand over so that I'm looking at the small lump under my skin.

"What? This is for the water credits."

Springer looks at me, shaking his head. "That's what they tell you. But think about it, Enora. How does that tracking device on your scope work? How does that data exist? Your tracer, well...it's their guarantee that anyone can be found. In our case, it ensures that there are no mistakes when it comes to an identified target."

I look at him and feel the horror that must be plastered on my face. "Are they always tracking me? Is everyone being tracked?" I look around me, imagining every person in the country being monitored by some unknown watcher. It's so invasive. My skin crawls just imagining it.

Springer lets out a breath. "I'm sure they could, but the tracers are only activated when required, like when they need to pinpoint our location during a mission or when intelligence data has indicated a terrorist. It would be way too taxing on the system to be tracking everyone at all times. But the point is that they can, at any time. For any reason."

I run my fingers over the evidence of this all-seeing eye and have an urge to rip it out. It has always been an essential part of my survival in a community. But now, that tiny square tucked under my skin feels menacing.

Springer clamps a hand over mine, stopping the incessant circling of my tracer. "This is no different than it was five minutes ago, Enora."

"Yes, it is!" How can he not see this?

"No. It's still your connection to this world. Think about how many times a day you pass your arm through a scanner. Consider how often you did that living in Prineville. Nothing has changed. You just understand its full capabilities now."

"But it's wrong!"

"Why?"

"Because...because there shouldn't be someone just watching me all the time." I feel indignant looking at him. He's so casual about it all.

"Do you think they don't watch you now? How many cameras are installed in the center? Do you even know? Someone is always watching."

I picture the training compound and can recall numerous cameras dotting the grounds, from the training yards to the quad. I see his point but I'm not ready to concede.

"If we couldn't use this device to track the guilty then you can be assured innocent people would die. Are you saying that your privacy is worth more than someone's life?"

He's always so logical. It's infuriating. While I want to hold onto my outrage, he has a point and it's hard to argue with him when he's throwing my own worry back in my face. "I didn't consider that."

"Perhaps you should. We're here to protect the innocent. Tracers help us do that."

I let out a sigh of defeat. "All right, all right, you've made your point. But don't you resent it? Just a little?"

Springer looks at me with a hard stare. "Yeah. But I can't change it and since it's a reality, I'm going to use it to do some good."

I force myself to let this go and focus on my training.

The remainder of the afternoon includes learning

additional features of my new scope and then a brief test of the communications information that I had been given earlier in the day. I know I score well and I also know that Springer will be reporting back to Bram. Bram, that's a whole other issue that I will need to sort out and I just can't face it right now.

The training ends and Springer walks me to the exit. I slide my arm in the reader and the door opens, but before I leave, Springer pulls my arm, leans close to my ear, and whispers, "You have to stick with the program, Enora. There's no other way. This world is at a breaking point. You've seen the data on water resources. You know what it means. I wish I could make you understand, but just trust me, there's no way out of this."

He lets go of my arm and I stand there frozen for a moment before I pull myself together and head out of the building. As I walk alone to the dorm, I think about what Springer said. There's more to it than the words themselves and I wonder at the meaning behind them.

I SPEND THE NEXT FEW WEEKS WORKING WITH Springer, learning all I can about being a Pathfinder, my one goal being finding a path out, out of all of this. To that end, I set aside my heart and embrace my position. Springer says nothing, nor does he allude to his warning. He accepts my efforts and works to continue shaping me into an effective weapon. But there's always something he's holding back, a piece of my training that he keeps tucked inside.

My new equipment is surprisingly hard for me to master. While I feel confident in my use of the basic scope and mapping software that I began with, this upgraded technology is taxing on my brain, the visuals alone are doing a number on my eyes and leaving me with blistering headaches. One such episode is so awful that a wave of nausea sweeps over me and I find myself flat on my back, having blacked out.

Springer is leaning over me and I feel him brush a tissue under my nose while asking, "Hey, you okay?"

My ears are ringing and I take a few moments to process his words before I can respond. "What happened?"

"You blacked out." He says, unconcerned. "It happens, no need to worry. I've seen it plenty of times when new Pathfinders are working with the programming."

He sweeps the tissue under my nose again. "Why are you wiping snot off my face?" I ask, vaguely embarrassed.

His eyes crinkle in a smile. "Just so you know, I wouldn't wipe your snotty nose. You've got a nosebleed, that's all."

My eyes skip to the tissue and I can see the blood. "What the hell?" I ask, suddenly pissed off that I've got the mother of all headaches and a bloody nose.

He laughs at my outrage and says, "Come on, I'll take you to the infirmary."

He helps me to my feet and we make our way to the nurse, a large woman who takes one look at me, rolls her eyes, and says, "Let me guess, new Pathfinder?"

I simply stare at her, too out of it to do anything but meekly sit where she tells me and submit to a quick examination. And so the training goes, until the headaches finally cease and I have fully integrated myself with the technology of my equipment.

Inevitably, the day comes when Bram enters our training session and informs us that we have been cleared for assignments in the field. I know what this means and I feel an inner battle begin to stir.

I walk to the wall of windows that overlook the new recruit training grounds. Outside these walls is an army in training. I can only speculate on the outcome of a single operation I may be assigned to and the impetus behind it. How many other assignments are conducted across the country? I am a part of something that I don't fully understand because there is only so much information I am given. I live in a realm of half-truths and harsh consequences. While my actions within the DMC will protect the innocent, there is a cost and that price is a piece of me.

I feel somewhat disconnected between what I was and what I have become. The ties that were cut the day I boarded the shuttle have left me without an anchor to my life. I am drifting, becoming unknown even to myself. And now I am on a precipice. If I do this thing, I will be letting go of part of my humanity. I will be like Bram, on a path to becoming a shell of who I was.

Springer comes up behind me and just stands quietly as if on some level he understands my inner turmoil. Minutes pass and I wait for him to speak, but he doesn't. He just stares out the same windows, lost in his own thoughts or simply observing the recruits beyond the glass. I am a rat in a maze. And that cheese at the end represents a life of privilege, if only I turn my back on my humanity.

I can't see my way forward and don't see a way out. And even if I could move on, outside is the next crop of fresh faces that will take my place. I don't fight it when a tear trails down my cheek. It takes some time to let it all go, this uncertainty and angst, but after a while I hang my head and whisper, "All right. Show me more."

The enemy
Is not on the battlefield
A soldier
Among the ranks
Gun in hand
And death in his heart
Rather, he is in me
And in the end
I must face him

CHAPTER ELEVEN

The next couple of weeks bring with them a sense of normalcy and routine. I have learned to anticipate Springer's moves which makes my job more efficient. Despite my aversion to them, I have also become adept at using a weapon. Springer took my frame and strength into account when he selected a gun for me to carry. It's small and black, holding a clip with fifteen rounds. I now find myself spending the first hour after lunch dismantling, cleaning, assembling, loading, and firing at a target; all under the watchful eyes of my counterpart. While Springer assures me that knowing how to operate a gun is purely a precaution, I wonder if I could actually fire it.

I haven't seen Bram since and for that I am grateful. I am not sure how to act around him and, frankly, I feel resentment over my situation and place a certain amount of blame at his feet. Though I know that this is rather unjustified, there it is. I also know the next time I see him will be to hear about my first real assignment. Delaying that inevitability is my hope.

I miss Drake when I can't escape my dorm to meet him at night. Since my encounter with Lina, and the warning from Rafe, I've been extra vigilant. This has meant a few occasions that left me stuck in bed, unable to risk sneaking out. I feel like I am being watched. For all I know, I am.

I finally catch a break, after three unsuccessful attempts to meet. Lina falls asleep quickly, having been worn out from some field exercise she complained loudly about while preparing for bed. Her voice grates on my nerves these days. It's become a sound that radiates up my spine when I hear it. I never used to feel that way.

As I dart down the halls, trying to look inconspicuous and probably failing miserably, I keep looking behind me, sure that I will see Lina's stare following my progress. I let out a deep breath when I make it to our rendezvous and see Drake's face light up when he spots me. He grabs my hand and pulls me into the tight quarters of the closet, shutting the door softly.

It feels safer once I am within the confines of this space. Drake gives me a quick hug, my heart thunders at the contact and I peek up at him, sure that he must be able to hear it.

"I've missed you," he whispers while tucking a stray clump of hair behind my ear. For a moment, I'm back on the hill and it's Bram's fingers combing through the strands. I blink my eyes slowly to dispel the image.

"I missed you, too. Lina's been on my ass, watching me like some stalker. If she hadn't had a grueling day in the field, I don't think I would've made it."

"Well then, I'm glad she got her ass kicked with whatever shit they had her doing." I can't help grinning at the huge smile that follows his remark.

We sit down and just lean into each other for a few minutes, content to just be in the moment.

Drake breaks the silence first. "So, I hear your Sweeper is Springer."

"Yeah, you heard of him?"

"Not really, just heard Rafe talking about him during a recent training. Apparently, Springer has quite a reputation. He's pretty well known in the unit. At least, that's the impression I got listening to Rafe."

I nod. It makes sense that he would have a name for himself. "I don't know him too well yet, but he seems like a good guy. He sure knows his stuff."

"You go out into the field yet?"

It makes me uneasy to have Drake ask me this. I've always assumed that the fieldwork is pretty confidential. Thankfully I don't have anything to share, but even if I did I'm not sure I would. I think it would feel wrong. "Not yet. What's going on with you? Is there talk of when you'll get paired with a Sweeper?"

"Nothing yet." This surprises me, as his skill was

comparable to mine when we trained together. He gives a small shrug. "I guess I just don't have your instincts."

I remain silent, thinking about what I recall from our time together. I suppose that there is truth in what he says, but I wonder if there is more to my rather fast promotion and his slower progress.

And then he says something startling. "Maybe the Commander pulled some strings or something to move you up so fast." His brows crease in thought. "Although, why the hell would he do that?"

Drake sighs. "Don't mind me. I don't know what the hell I'm saying. It doesn't matter anyway. I'm in no real rush to put these skills into action, and I honestly don't know if I'll be able to when the time comes anyway."

"You will," I whisper.

Thank God he can't see my face. Could Bram be behind this? It is a disturbing thought, though one that may have some merit. I'll need to ask Springer. But the next morning I don't get a chance to.

As soon as I arrive at my unit, Springer announces that we need to pack up and be ready to leave in thirty minutes. We will be traveling by jeep to a location four hours away. I quickly get to work, setting aside all thoughts of Bram. Four hours away. I review in my head what locations might be in that vicinity, but until I get more details, it's just guesswork.

Springer steps out for a few minutes and returns with food and water rations. I decide that it is a really good thing that he is in charge because it's all I can do to get my meager supplies ready, much less think about the big picture of what we may need. After thirty minutes, we are heading to the quad where a jeep is waiting. Up to this point I have still not heard any details about the assignment, which worries me. I have a feeling that he's waiting until we are on the way before dropping the bomb.

The jeep pulls out of the compound and we head east. It feels good to have the wind blowing in my face, it's cleansing. I let the miles go by, content to just enjoy to the freedom, before I ask for details. "So, where are we headed?"

"Brigford."

"Brigford?" My voice sounds loud to my ears. I've only seen cities on the screen and everything I've heard has made me so thankful to be in a small town. It's a bit intimidating to visit a place that is often the site of riots and viral outbreaks.

"Yeah, Brigford."

Brigford is a huge city, eclipsing Prineville. I feel pangs of anxiety as I imagine how challenging it will be to map it. No training exercise has had the myriad of complications that a large urban area possesses and suddenly I realize that I am not ready for this.

Springer must have a sixth sense when it comes to me

because he says, "Don't worry, Enora, you're not expected to map the whole city. We won't be the only team."

While I know this should ease my mind, it doesn't. "You still haven't given me any specifics. What's the assignment? Surveillance?" It's a foolish idea, but I can't help saying it in the hope that by voicing the idea it'll become a reality.

I want him to say yes, but deep down I know he won't. In the end it's the hesitation that tells me all I need to know. Reality is always so much uglier than what I imagine.

"No, we will not be setting up surveillance." Springer pauses. "There is a faction of rebellion that has been growing in the city. The information we have indicates they are planning an attack within the city though we do not have knowledge of when and where. Intelligence data has identified three meeting places the group has used recently. We have been assigned to one of the locations."

"What's going to happen if they are in our location?"

Springer turns to me, his eyes cold with the knowledge of what is inevitable. "They will be eliminated."

I can't do this. I feel panic building inside me. This is different than Clearcreek. At least there I found out after and didn't have to see anything in real time. I clench my hand on the armrest and try to pull myself together. Come on, Enora. Think about the greater good. You don't know what these people are planning. You and Springer could save hundreds of civilians. I eventually talk myself down, but the uncertainty lingers.

"Springer?"

"Yeah?"

"I...I don't know if I can do this. You know, when the time comes." I look at his profile to gauge his reaction.

"You can and you will."

I shake my head in denial. "What if I can't? I mean, why are they being targeted? Is there something awful being planned that could hurt innocent people?"

"You know I'm not always provided that information. We've talked about this, Enora."

"I know, it's just...it feels wrong, you know?"

He glances at me for a moment before returning his eyes to the road. "I get it. Believe me, I understand. But this is the job we have to do."

He's so matter-of-fact that a bubble of resentment floats to the surface of my thoughts. "That's so callous! These are people too. Shouldn't they have a say?"

"How do you know they didn't? What if there is intelligence data that indicates a massive attack? What if they are going to target a school or public square to make some kind of statement?"

He has a point. Springer told me we're the good guys in all of this, and I need to believe that. I sigh, accepting his implication of some rationale for our assignment, and look out the window at the barren landscape. "You know, sometimes I wish I could just run away from this, all of it.

The cracked earth and hard living. Just go somewhere, a place they wouldn't be able to find me."

"And what about me?" Springer asks quietly. "What do you think they would do to me if you ran?"

He knows I'm not serious about running, but the point is made and I'm ashamed not to have considered it. I hadn't given a thought to Springer. Horrible images chase through my head of torture and execution. I feel that noose around my neck tightening. It's all so perfectly orchestrated. They made me care about him and now he's a weapon to use against me.

It is such a claustrophobic feeling, to know that even if I felt desperate enough, I could do nothing. I couldn't bear the weight of the guilt that I would feel should Springer be punished because of me.

I lean my head against the seat and watch the landscape pass by. The scenery rarely changes and, aside from a few vultures, I see few signs of life. This is the bleak reality that I need to face. Beyond the fence of every community is nothing. No water, no food, no chance of survival. The Company knows this, depends on it. I suppose that there are some who live beyond the borders. God knows not everyone was rounded up as the Company swept through, but where those people live and how they live is beyond my imagining.

As we continue along the bumpy road, I see broken down bits of the past dotting the landscape. Old houses and stores, just shells now, overgrown with weeds and decay. The sky is a brilliant blue, its beauty almost eclipsing the barren ugliness of the earth. There are only a few cars we pass on the road. Our training center is on the small side and the other teams joining us in Brigford are coming from another location. For the most part, we are alone. I have never felt so alone, as though I could just disappear in a wisp of smoke and no one would know.

Two hours into the drive we pull over to stretch our legs. Rolling brown hills are peppered with scraggly trees and bushes. The road we are traveling on has seen better days. We must be taking a back route to the city, because I know that main roads are well maintained by the DMC. The internal battle is still raging inside my head over what I will be a part of once we reach the city. But like before, I don't see a way out.

Standing in the dirt and looking at the hillside, I begin to realize that I have never been so free. Never before have I been so far out the range of the Company's eyes. It is like a balm on the open wounds that I feel. I take a deep breath, imagining that the air tastes different, that it tastes of freedom. I can feel Springer watching me.

I turn to him. "Do you feel it?"

"Feel what?"

I open my arms to the burning sky. "Freedom."

He cocks his head as though needing elaboration. And I continue, "No one is watching us. I mean we could just drive off and no one would know. We could be free."

Springer saunters toward me until he is less than a foot

away. I can feel his breath on my face as I look up into his eyes. He lifts his arm, curling his hand behind my neck, then leans into my ear.

"But they do know."

His fingers stroke the small lump on the inside of my wrist. "We're never free, Enora," his voice whispers. For a moment I forgot about that, my own tracer.

How deceiving it is, this wide-open space I see around me. I simply can't see the bars of my cage, but they are there, invisible yet just as confining and with their hidden nature, more menacing. Springer walks a few paces away, leaving me to come to terms with this new reality. I look up into the sky and see a black shape soaring in the distance. The wingspan is huge as it circles hundreds of feet above the earth. It can only be a vulture, but even that often-despised scavenger looks beautiful in my eyes. What I wouldn't give to be free like that bird.

I shift my attention back to the dry, hard ground and crouch in the shade of the jeep. My hands hang limply, dangling above my feet as I rest my arms on my knees. My tracking device, how could I have forgotten that insidious device?

"Do you think they're watching us now?" My voice is soft, belying my anger.

"Yes." Springer crouches next to me and chucks a small pebble. "I would imagine our tracers were activated the moment we left the compound and that they've been tracking us since."

I squint my eyes in the glare of the sun. We sit in silence for a few minutes before facing the inevitable and climbing back into the jeep. Another hour into the drive and we begin to see signs that we are coming closer to the city.

In the distance I see the outline of what I assume is a stockyard. The multiple buildings are long with white roofs and barred openings along the sides. On the breeze I catch a faint smell that I have never encountered before. It is an earthy scent with a sour undertone that makes me wrinkle my nose in distaste. I can only wonder what animals create such a smell and am thankful when the breeze from my open window shifts, taking the stink away. Along the perimeter of the buildings I can clearly see the heavily guarded fence. Looking at the guard towers, I wonder who may have been desperate enough to attempt to breach this tight security and if so, how long they lasted before they were taken down.

A few more miles up the road I see another cluster of buildings but these have distinct features that are indicative of a large greenhouse with surrounding fields of crops. I gaze at the rows and rows of plants in the fields and wonder what type of food is being grown. I have no concrete knowledge of what food producing plants look like, unless you count Safa's seedlings, and I suddenly feel so ignorant. Shouldn't I know these things? I shake my head in frustration.

Then my eyes widen as I see what looks like a band of

colors just above the rows of plants. It fades briefly and then I see it again. It is the most beautiful thing I have ever seen. I can see it glisten in the light of the sun, displaying a brilliant array of color. Springer must have noted my attention because he slows the jeep to a crawl so that I can gaze upon this new wonder a bit longer.

"It's a rainbow."

I continue looking at this phenomenon and roll the word around in my head trying to place it into a context that I am familiar with. I vaguely recall having heard of a rainbow, but until this moment what I was told and what I am looking at are two entirely different things. Light refraction comes to mind, but I am hard pressed to compare that dry term to what I am seeing.

Springer interrupts my thoughts by stopping the jeep. "Do you see how the colors fade and then return?" I bob my head as I keep staring. "There are jets of water being sprayed over the fields of plants. The rainbow is created when the water and the rays of the sun are at just the right angle."

Water. This is the missing component for me. How can there be rainbows when the rain is so infrequent and sprays of water in the sunlight unheard of? I watch the rainbows appear and fade and wonder how many water rations each plant is getting. From what I can see, the plants get far more water than the people of Prineville. It seems like an injustice.

CHAPTER TWELVE

Brigford is not what I had imagined. I knew about the concrete walls erected around large cities to both keep in and keep out, but to see it in person, rather than on a screen, is jarring. The walls are so high that I have to crane my neck to see the top of them. Along the top of the walls are dozens of intermittent towers manned by at least two Sentinels each. It is a forbidding sight.

We come to an entrance point in the wall and stop as a Sentinel comes forward. His uniform is familiar, like those I have seen throughout my childhood. The only distinguishing feature is the man himself. His square face has a large jaw which seems to flow into the thickest neck I have ever seen. His shoulders are massively wide and the pads of muscle along his chest and arms make him look almost freakishly big. The deep voice that rumbles from his mouth only completes the picture.

"Credentials?" he gruffly asks.

I am more than willing to let Springer handle this situation and keep my mouth shut as he briefly explains that we have business within the city limits. The guard looks dubious and brings out a portable scanner to verify our privileges. I hold out my arm almost wishing that we are denied access, but today is not my day for wishes to come true. Within moments we are saluted and then, what can only be described as the jaws of hell, open before us and reveal the city.

My first impression is one of darkness. It feels as if the sun has been blocked from the sky and all is in shadow. The buildings are so numerous and so tall that I can hardly conceptualize how many people are meant to live here. As we drive through the winding maze of streets, I notice that there is a distinct difference between those buildings that were produced by the Company and those that are of the past. I see structures of brick and stone with curves and character that I have not seen before, juxtaposed with structures that are like elongated modulars from my town. As we pass building after building, I begin to wonder how many people live in this city and how they survive. I see neither factories nor training centers. What does everyone do to earn credits?

It is as I am mulling this over that my conscious thought pieces together what I am seeing, and I answer my own question. There are no people. The part of the city we are driving through is a ghostly shell. It is with this realization that I look a little harder at the buildings that had so impressed me a moment ago and see the worn facades and the crumbling brick. Windows in both the newer and older structures are clouded with age and many are simply broken. Clearly, this part of the city has long been empty, and I don't have to wonder about the reasons too long when I see evidence of the decay and desperation in an alley between two of the abandoned structures.

Movement catches my eye and I turn my head, trying to get a clearer view. At first glance, they look like dogs fighting in the street, an unheard of sight in itself as the only dogs I have ever seen are those that are part of the DMC security teams. But they are not dogs. They are men. Springer follows my line of sight and stops the jeep, seeming just as interested in what is going on in the dim shadows as I am.

I am unable to see what the men are fighting over until a bottle is suddenly knocked out of a hand, hitting the ground and rolling a few feet beyond the struggling pair. Then I hear a familiar whistle, shrill and ear-piercing, as a Sentinel comes charging down the opposite end of the alley, weapon drawn. The men instantly stop struggling and run for the shadows. They don't make it very far. A bolt of electricity from a taser passes through them, sending them crashing to the ground. Their bodies twitch spastically. I look away, my eyes resting on the bottle. I watch the water slowly leak from it, disappearing into the dusty ground.

Aside from some random security teams and the few pockets of sparse community, we see no further signs of life. It is when we reach another checkpoint that I begin to realize the city has been systematically downsized. It reminds me of a target, like those I used in training, with rings that ended in the center, the bulls-eye. I wonder what is in the heart of this ghost town.

Passing through the second checkpoint, I see a subtle change in the structures and inhabitants. It is cleaner, newer, and more populated. But it remains clear to me that this part of the city once held many more people than it does now. I can't help thinking about the newscasts I grew up watching, those images of disease, fighting, and riots that plagued cities. I see nothing of this now and begin to wonder why, but in my heart I know the answer: there simply aren't enough people to riot, aren't enough people to spread plagues.

I look over at Springer and see his attention focused on a building to the right. He slows the jeep, makes a sharp turn and heads straight for the wall. My eyes bulge and my hands reflexively shoot forward, bracing my body against the dash. A scream is about to bubble up when the wall shifts, opening a large passageway, and we dip down into the darkness. I crane my neck and look behind me as we pass through the wall, watching it close and thinking that I have just been swallowed.

The jeep has stopped, and I can see nothing. Springer flips on a flashlight and as my eyes adjust I realize that we are in what looks like an old, underground parking lot. Springer looks over and says, "This is the rendezvous point for all of the teams."

"Oh," is all I can utter as my heart decelerates and I work to calm myself.

"Grab your pack and let's head up to the fifth level." Springer is so matter-of-fact, that it immediately puts me at ease and I hop out of the jeep to get my gear.

I follow him up the first flight of stairs and then see light from outside illuminating the stairwell. "Is this building occupied by civilians?"

He pauses. "There are a few residents on the first floor, but the remainder of the building is vacant. Most of the buildings in the city are occupied in the same way until you get to the epicenter."

"How is it different there?"

Springer stops, one foot resting on the next step. "Have you noticed how empty the city is?"

"I'm not blind."

"But have you considered what this place, the world for that matter, looked like before?"

I nod. "I was thinking about it on the drive in. I mean, if this is just one city that probably had a population that was a couple hundred thousand, then wouldn't the world-wide population have been like tens of millions? I'm guessing at least half died from the drought and wars and such."

"Billions died." He pauses to let that number sink in. "There were about eight billion people in the world when the drought first hit. Today, it's maybe ten million."

The number is staggering. I take in the buildings with a new perspective. "So, how many people lived here?"

Springer cocks his head, thinking. "I'd guess about four million and I bet there's not even a tenth of that now."

My jaw drops. "Millions of people once lived in this city and now only thousands." Saying it makes it seem more real somehow, but it's still an intangible idea.

"That population makes up the bulk of Brigford. The central district of the city, Renascence, has a much smaller populace. I'm guessing just a couple thousand."

In my head I'm imaging an aerial view of the city with a small community at its heart. "Why is there a separate area within the city? Why isn't it just part of Brigford?"

"It's different there, not like what we're driving through."

"What do you mean, different?" I can tell he's leaving something out the way he's not looking right at me.

Springer shrugs. "It's hard to describe. I've only seen it once and even, then I didn't spend more than a few hours there. It's just different. Newer somehow and..." but he doesn't finish, just shakes his head.

"What?" Why is he being so weird about it?

"It's not important. Just trust me, Renascence is like a separate place within all of this." He hustles me past a large building that's seen better days. "Come on. We better hustle."

There are two other teams in the room. I look each individual over, noting the age, build, and ease with which they sit there discussing an assassination. My stomach churns. It is evident that these teams have done this before, many times. There are three men and only one other girl, a woman actually. They are lean and wiry like us and their eyes are hard, like they have seen too much. My parents always said that the eyes are the mirrors of your soul. When I look into the woman's eyes, there is no soul reflected there. They are empty, devoid of any emotion, lifeless. I am looking at myself in the future and it frightens me.

Two of the men are Pathfinders, Jasper and Maddox. Jade and Flynn are their counterparts, Sweepers. Each team has taken on a preparatory role prior to our arrival, Jasper and Flynn have been conducting a surveillance of the potential locations, while Maddox and Jade have scouted out the best vantage points for the Pathfinders. It is decided that we will commence at one in the morning after intelligence information indicates that the targets would be meeting close to that time. The only piece of information that is unknown is the exact location of this meeting, hence the need for multiple teams. The assignment is simple: monitor identified tracers to location and eliminate all targets. Once the assignment is complete, alert the Cleaners.

Springer and I are assigned to a building just beyond the third checkpoint, on the fringes of the heart of the city. I am eager to go for the simple reason that I cannot bear to be in the same room as the woman, Jade. I can't stop looking at her and thinking about what this job is going to turn me into. It makes me wonder if she was once like me. Did she ever fight this? Did it slowly eat away at who she was until there was nothing left, just the shell I see now? Or did she want to be their monster? I leave all of my questions behind as we grab our gear and leave the building.

Springer leads us through a maze of alleys until we are just outside the third checkpoint. The sky is darkening, but the illumination from the city center casts false light making it seem much earlier. We duck into an abandoned building and head to the eastern corner of the top floor. I walk to the set of windows that overlooks the checkpoint and the city center beyond and use my arm to wipe away years of dust. Springer is quiet, standing beside me, as I look out at the city below.

It is different, just like he said. My eyes swell as I take in what can only be described as a gluttonous mass of opulence compared to the decay just beyond the wall. In the center are paths cutting through green carpets that must be grass, though I can't be sure as I've never seen any that lush. A fountain sits in the middle, where the paths intersect. My gaze feels glued to this sight. I watch, mesmerized, as water gently flows out of it, cascading into a pool. I have a hard time tearing my eyes away from it.

I see people moving about, so many more people compared to the sparse numbers outside the thick barriers. And I finally understand. This is why they are fighting, that nameless, faceless group of people I will be hunting. It is because of this, this small mass of humanity that was somehow selected as the elite, the lucky ones. From the look of their dwellings, they must have abundant food, new clothing, and ample water credits. I bet they don't wake up to dust in their mouths and nostrils and dirt caked under their nails. I feel my hands clenching as I continue to watch life in utopia unfold before me. Resentment builds to anger when I think about Safa. She was violently arrested for using a few cups of water for her tiny garden. Cups! And here, there is a fountain. It is so unfair.

I turn my head, anger making my heart thunder in my ears, and look at Springer.

"I can't do this. I won't."

He looks down at me, his mouth down turned. "You will, Enora."

Rage flows out of me as I swing my arm to encompass the whole view. "No! Look at this! How can I even think about killing someone who wants to fight this? I want to fight it!" Tears of anger course down my cheeks. "How can you just stand there and be okay with this?"

Springer looks out the window. "Because I have to,

Enora. Because there is no choice, not for me," he turns to me and looks deeply into my eyes. "And not for you. What do you think would happen to your parents if you refused to perform your duties?"

A hoarse sob escapes as I turn my back on the scene below and collapse onto the floor, my fisted hands wrapped around my head. I am a rat in a maze, only this maze has no way out.

I don't know how long I have been sitting on the floor, but eventually I raise my head and look up at Springer who is still standing at the window, looking out.

"I know how you are feeling, Enora. I felt it too when I saw it for the first time." He looks down at me, understanding reflected in his gaze. Understanding and something else: resignation and determination. He turns back to the window.

"We have a job to do."

My voice has only a slight tremor as I ask, "Don't you mean we have people to murder?"

His head jerks toward me, shock momentarily registering on his face before he wipes it clean, clenches his teeth and says, "Get your scope set up and then get some rest. You have two hours."

I watch as he walks away and settles himself in the other room. I feel utterly alone and bound in invisible iron manacles that force my hands to grope for my scope and robotically prepare for tonight.

CHAPTER THIRTEEN

Springer has been gone for thirty minutes when I hear his voice in the microphone in my ear. "I'm at the point of origin."

I nod reflexively, knowing he can't see me, but somehow it helps keep my hands from shaking as I continue to grapple with what I am a part of and what I can't escape. I must do this. I shake out my hands, trying to get rid of the residual tremors, wipe my sweaty palms on my slacks and put my eyes to the scope.

Twenty minutes pass and the tracers show no movement. A sigh of relief escapes, but it's premature. One by one, the targets begin to move. I can see the blips on the screen traveling from multiple directions as the tracking program monitors the progress of the targets. Inside, I am praying that the innocent dots head toward one of the other teams but feel my heart stutter when they turn toward our location. I watch the tracers of the four individuals enter the building we have been assigned to.

"No go. Not all targets at location." There should be five tracers. I scan the surrounding area and see that one, at the farthest location, has remained behind. I am prepared for this scenario. We can't complete the assignment unless all targets are at one location. It's too risky to leave anyone behind. I can't deny my sense of relief, even though I know I'll have to await another opportunity.

"Copy. Returning to you."

And then I see movement. Crap. "Hold. Target on the move." I watch the fifth individual quickly move to the rendezvous.

At this point, I switch to an infrared setting so that I can monitor their movements more precisely within the structure. They eventually stop in an upper level. I know it's time to tell Springer his access point and their location, but I feel like the words are stuck in my throat.

"Location?"

It is as if I am standing outside myself, listening to my voice as it whispers, "Five in the western corner of the sixth floor."

There is stillness for the span of a few rapid heartbeats and then, "Copy, on my way. Shadow me."

I flip off the infrared and switch back to the tracking system. Homing in on the point of origin, I see Springer emerge. I take stock of which path he is taking, quickly scan for any civilians and reply, "Clear."

All too soon he reaches the building where the targets have been located. I switch again to infrared and follow him as he begins the ascent to the upper floor. Every few seconds, I shift the scope to scan the area where the targets are, ensuring that no one has moved or heard Springer. My pulse is racing and I begin to sweat as he gets closer to the sixth floor. I can hear myself panting at the same rate that I hear Springer's breathing as he silently runs up the flights of stairs. And then he is there, three rooms down, in a hallway. I can see him stopped, perhaps listening.

I whisper, "Clear."

And then watch with mounting dread and he walks slowly down the hall and stops outside the door.

He looks over at me then, well not really looking at me, but I see his head turn in my direction, see the sockets of his eyes look at me, and then he enters the room. There is a pause, no more than a second, but it's there, and then all I can hear in my earpiece is shouting and the muffled bang of his gun followed by the horrible thud of a body hitting the floor. It is over quickly.

His voice cracks. "Clear. Alert the Cleaners. Returning to you."

I continue to look through my scope in a state of shock. The bodies are still glowing with heat, though none are moving. I just look, paralyzed by the horror of what I have done. I'm still looking through the scope at the slowly cooling bodies when Springer reaches past me and pulls my scope away from the window.

My brain clicks into gear and I turn to him. "You paused when you went through the door. Why did you pause?"

I see him gulp, and then he steps away from me, slowly sinks to his knees. His head is hanging as I reach out my hand and touch his back. I don't say anything, wouldn't know what to say anyway. My palm just rests between his shoulder blades, silent testimony to my loyalty, and my understanding. Eventually he slides himself backward and rests against the wall. His head is resting face-down on his bent knees. I wait for him to speak.

"They were young. Too young." He turns troubled eyes to me. "Young like you, Enora, maybe even younger. I've never..." He stops, shaking his head, trying to capture the right words. "It's never been like this. They've always been older, aware of the risks, but this...this was just killing children." I ease myself next to him and just sit, offering my silent support. I don't feel like one of the 'good guys'.

All is not as it seems
Though the outer skin
Lies smooth and flawless
Just beneath
Lying in wait under the surface
Decay is spreading
A festering sore
About to burst

CHAPTER FOURTEEN

It's a strange homecoming when we return to the training center, very subdued. Springer and I spent most of the drive in contemplative silence, which carries over into our arrival and subsequent unpacking. There is no aura of celebration, though having completed our first assignment in the field I suppose there ought to be.

Bram comes into our room, as we are our cleaning and putting away equipment. "Congratulations on the successful completion of your first assignment." He looks at both of us, oozing sincerity. I feel a little queasy hearing it. "Your work was exceptional, and I hear from the other teams that you were both professional and efficient."

Springer straightens from his crouch on the floor and walks to Bram, holding out his hand. "Thank you, Commander." They shake hands, both smiling, though I know Springer's grin is fake.

I take my cue from Springer and extend my own hand, ready to show appreciation for a compliment that feels wrong. Bram's firm grip engulfs my hand, warm and disturbingly familiar. "You are on your way to a successful career as a Pathfinder, Enora. Keep up the good work."

"I will do my best, Commander." I look in his eyes as I say this, wanting to see some glimpse of the boy I knew, the one who would've been horrified by the deaths of children in the name of preserving peace. But there's nothing, only a sincere belief in our righteous defense of society. I can't help the sinking sensation in my heart.

"Enjoy a well-earned respite this afternoon. I will see you both soon, for your next assignment." He nods and walks out the door. The room is silent for a few moments as Springer and I just stare at the empty doorway.

I hear Springer clear his throat. "Let's finish up and then you can have some downtime."

Though a part of me wants to, we don't talk about what happened. That room. Who was there. How young they were. We don't talk about it and perhaps that's best, but it isn't. Not really.

So I just nod and get back to work.

NORMALCY RETURNS FOR A FEW DAYS, AS SPRINGER and I resume our exercises. It is the repetitive nature of the tasks I perform that allows me to distance myself from the events in Brigford. I know better than to bring them up, so

I smother the feelings and pretend I'm still one of the good guys.

We receive a summons four days after returning. I am ready for it. Springer had indicated it would likely happen within a week. So it is with no surprise that we walk into Bram's office and hear him say, "I'm happy to let you both know that your advancement for full-time fieldwork has been approved."

I try to put on an acceptable expression as Bram turns to me. "Enora, this is your opportunity to show the DMC what you are capable of. Success in this role has many benefits including better housing and food as well as increased credits for yourself and your family members."

It's hard to see the downside in this advancement when it means my parents will be better off. I know how much they struggled over the years. Each time I call lately, I can hear the effects of better housing and more water credits in their voices. While the cost of this is high, I know I can do it for them. It only hurts a little to smile and respond to Bram's explanation. "I appreciate your faith in me and won't let you down."

Springer adds his own comment, solidifying my part in this. "Enora has proven herself already and I am sure she will advance quickly to improved status, Commander."

"Very good." Bram reaches out and shakes our hands before we leave. Each encounter is like this now, so formal and devoid of feeling. It's hard for me to stop comparing my interactions with Bram to how it used to be. I don't know that I'll ever really get used to who he is now. I'm not sure that I really want to. As I walk out of the room, I try to ignore the fact that I have agreed to kill people in exchange for a nicer bed and better food. I'm not entirely successful.

It's hard to meet Drake's eyes when I encounter him that evening. I see his face split into that smile that I've missed, but it quickly falters when he looks at me as I try valiantly to paste a smile in return. Seeing him makes it too easy to lose my grip on my emotions and break down. So I hold up my hand to block his progress when his eyes look worried and his arms begin to open in an offer of embrace. I shake my head and silently plead with him, begging him to help me keep up my façade so that I don't break down. I see him mouth the word, *later?* And I nod.

But when later arrives I find myself unable to let go of the waves of emotion that I have locked inside myself. Drake asks me quietly to explain what happened, but I shake my head fearing that if I let it out I won't be able to stop.

"I can't, Drake, I just..." my head shakes my denial and I rest my cheek against his chest.

I feel his arms go around me and I sink into his warmth, letting my worry go and focusing on the present. In the end I don't tell him anything. I find that I just can't speak the words. It would make it too real if I utter them and I need to lock up those thoughts and memories or I know I will find myself lost or crazy.

The next day Drake is sent off on his own assignment and I find a measure of relief in this. It is just too hard to bottle it all up when we are together, and I don't want to face it. Like a door, I close that experience and don't think about it, and decide to throw myself into the training that Springer and I are completing, putting all of my energy and focus into learning about the new devices I will need to master. I know that it is a fragile peace that I feel as I focus on our work and that soon enough I will be put to another test.

"You're pretty damn good, you know that?"

Springer's compliment surprises me and I find myself smiling with a measure of pride.

"Thanks."

We have just finished our training for the day and are packing up our equipment before heading back to our common areas. I'm particularly cautious with the new scanner I have been working with. It enables me to scan an enclosed space and add it to a mapping file data bank. When I put each data scan together, I have a complete schematic of an underground area. In order to learn and test the equipment, Springer has taken me to various locations below ground level; areas I never knew existed, as their entry points are restricted. As I continue to collect and store my gear, I feel Springer's eyes on me and turn to catch him looking, surprised when he doesn't try to disguise his stare.

"What?" I ask in a somewhat accusing tone.

He shrugs. "Nothing." I see him mull over his next comment. "Want to take a walk for a bit?"

"Sure."

We head out of the building and toward the perimeter fence where a guard is standing at a side gate. I turn my head to look at Springer, silently questioning why he isn't slowing, and then find the guard nodding and opening the gate. It's after training exercises are over and I am a bit stunned to find that we can just walk out. As we pass through the gate I can't help turning my head to make sure the guard doesn't suddenly come to his senses and begin to chase us down, but he is simply closing the gate, his attention on something else.

From the corner of my eye, I see Springer smirk. "What, did you think he was gonna tackle us to the ground or something for trying to escape?"

"You mean we can just walk out whenever we want?"

Springer grins. "Well, perhaps *you* can't yet but, yeah, I can pretty much leave when I want. Come on, let's head up there."

Twenty minutes later we find ourselves on the top of a rocky hill overlooking the grounds. We sit in silence for a time, just being there, no need to fill the quiet with idle chatter. As my body begins to relax, I feel awash in bitter-sweet memories. My eyes sting with tears as I remember another hill, in another time, with another warm arm gently brushing against mine. Things are so much different now than when Bram and I used to sit together, dreaming dreams and sharing secrets.

Springer clears his throat, as if giving me time to collect myself from my apparent nostalgia. "I know it's hard, Enora, but you've gotta hang in there."

It's like he can cut through all the bravado and bullshit, like an arrow that deftly pierces the heart through a chink in armor. I don't stop the tears that have pooled from falling. I know he won't judge me, and frankly, this is the only place where I can just let out my misery. He lets me be for a time, just sitting quietly while I pull myself together. My tears eventually run their course and I let them dry in the hot breeze, making pale tracks through the inevitable dirt on my cheeks.

"How do you do it, Springer? I mean, how do you just forget the horror and go on?"

"It doesn't ever leave me, Enora. I mean, it's not like I can simply shut it all away and never think about it." He takes a deep breath and exhales slowly. "I see their faces every night. I think I will always see their faces, and maybe it's better that way. What kind of person would I be if they meant nothing? What would it make me if I could just walk away and never give it a thought?"

Springer's face is turned away from me, gazing into the distance though I don't think he is really seeing the landscape ahead of him. "I guess I take them with me, because they are always there, all of them. More than you even know."

He swivels his head to look me in the eyes and I see the aching remorse buried in their depths and wonder how I could ever have believed that the ghosts of his past weren't there, lurking just beneath the surface.

He reaches up and brushes strands of hair from my face, tucking it behind my ear.

"I don't forget, but I can lock it away and go on because that is what I need to do, that is what you need to do. People like us, we don't get to choose, we don't have that luxury. So you just need to get through it, you got it? We just need to get the job done."

His eyes bore into mine as though he can force his words into my head so that I will capitulate and accept my fate, but I struggle against his coaxing arguments, unable to give in fully quite yet, though I understand his reasoning.

"I'm not there yet, Springer." Perhaps in time I can learn to acquiesce, but I'm feeling too raw and it feels too wrong.

"I get it, but you need to get your head wrapped around this. It's you and me, okay? We're a team and I've gotta know you're going to be there for me when I need you. Like I am here when you need me."

I don't respond as what he says sinks in. But my muscles relax, just a bit and I know he has marked this release of tension.

Springer sinks back onto his elbows, accepting my silent perspective and not wanting to push me to consent to his. It is an easy truce. He knows I'm not going anywhere, knows I'm too much of a coward to put up any real fight. The lion inside me wants to roar in revolution but is trapped just under the surface of my timid shell, not strong enough to emerge and release its wrath.

After a few minutes I ask, "How old are you?"

Springer chuckles. "What do you think?"

"Twenty?" He doesn't seem that much older than me, though I can see some hard living stamped on his face.

"Good guess. I'm twenty-two."

I watch his eyes drift to the sky, tracking the black outline of a bird. "Did you have another Pathfinder? I mean, before me?"

"Yeah."

I wait for him to go on, but he doesn't elaborate. "Did something happen?"

He leans forward and picks up a rock, gently tossing it from one hand to another. "We had been a team for about a year when he was ambushed. I was too far away to help."

"Oh." This is the first time I have really thought about any physical danger I may be in when working in the field. To me, it has always been Springer taking the big risks. "I'm sorry." I don't know what else to say. Silence descends,. We let time drift until the fading light signals it's time to go back.

CHAPTER FIFTEEN

It is a week later that Springer and I are back in Brigford, only this time I'm in the heart of the city. They call it Renascence, this epicenter of what was once a huge metropolis. It is essentially cut-off from the outlying areas of the city with all supply being sent directly through the only remaining monorail system, which has one terminal. It is surreal to enter through the heavily manned gate and find myself in a community so disparate from those outside the walls surrounding it.

We have been given a new directive, one that I am far more comfortable with, on the surface at least: mapping the old, underground tunnel systems. Prior to our departure, Springer was advised that it was recently discovered that the Renascence system had been hacked and information about the substructure of the micro-city corrupted. It is unknown when the hack occurred, meaning it could've been recent or months or even years ago and whatever information was stolen or altered could've been used for multiple purposes. We have been selected to covertly go in and investigate the tunnels while simultaneously generating a detailed schematic.

We have been outfitted differently for this assignment and I find myself in a new uniform. I am a Sentinel in the epicenter of the city. The shirt and slacks are a relentless black with black satin striping down the arms and legs and while I am dressed to blend in, I am anything but your typical Sentinel.

As I look around the headquarters, at the numerous black clad individuals, I am reminded of the hulking guard that we originally encountered at the outer wall. I let my gaze wander from one Sentinel to another and find that they all seem to possess similar physical traits. It is as though the Sentinels of the city are a special breed and in the back of my mind a seed of suspicion is planted.

Springer and I are assigned accommodation within Renascence headquarters. Through Bram, we have been provided with a viable reason for being here and our rank allows us some perks: freedom of movement within the city center and a private room. There are two beds in the room we will share but it is our own space. This allows us some privacy but in no way does it mean we are not being watched. We are always being watched and listened to, within these walls, within this micro city. That is one thing Springer had told me on the way here. I'm careful with what I say, making sure it is always pro-Company. With posters of General Malvolia dotting various hallways, it is impossible to forget.

Renascence is a newer creation, somewhere around forty years old, and its infrastructure was created with the intention of constant surveillance of the populace. I find it disturbing. There are multiple forms of surveillance throughout the city and within each building, everything from cameras to microphones. Each type of surveillance is computer-monitored. The entire system is coded with images and key words and phrases that will alert the system and deploy Sentinels to an identified location. It is nerve-wracking when I think about it and I begin to wonder if my own town had such technology, perhaps that would explain Safa's discovery and subsequent arrest. My only consolation is in the work Springer and I will be doing that will keep us out of that omniscient eye, at least until we complete our assignment.

This micro city is walled, like a fortress, complete with guard towers. I notice that unlike the outskirts of the metropolis, the buildings within Renascence are all reminiscent of our modern architecture with each style of dwelling progressing outward like rings of circles until the perimeter is reached. It is clear that while the multifamily dwellings closest to the wall are the least desirable, they are far nicer than the buildings outside of Renascence, and even those back home. I estimate the total area of this epicenter to be less than three square miles and is bordered on two sides by what were waterways, making the area more of an oval shape when thinking of it on a map.

While Renascence itself is an anomaly, there is something else about the community which makes me uneasy. Aside from the imposing girth of the Sentinels being themselves disquieting, I sense something that I can't identify, but is there nonetheless. I don't share my qualms with Springer, rather I watch and listen.

The creation of Renascence resulted in resentment from those people living outside its protective walls and beyond, making it a likely target for rebel factions. Multiple attempts to access and attack this sector of Brigford have been attempted over the years and persist today. Recent intelligence suggests that a terrorist group hacked into a databank of the city's schematics, potentially using this information to breach one of the subterranean tunnels upon which it is built to infiltrate Renascence. Now these access points are a threat and I am tasked with mapping the entire tunnel system and then installing concealed surveillance equipment which will be paired with the system already in place in the city. What happens after I am finished is not something I think about.

When I enter the tunnels, I think of Drake and the uranium mines that so many of the people in his town are condemned to. I haven't given him much thought since he left on his own assignment, but now I wonder where he is and what he is doing. I hope he is above ground somewhere because the ominous feeling of the tunnels is overwhelming. I can't imagine being forced to spend my life in such darkness.

The first day is the most grueling. I find myself jumping at shadows, my heart lurching each time some part of my body or Springer's blocks the light. As the hours pass, it is with a vague sense of disgust that I realize many of the tunnels were sewers, though my rational side tells me whatever once flowed through these passageways has long since dried up and crumbled to nothing, the other part of me wants to cringe away and scour my body to get it clean. I cannot imagine a whole city flushing so much waste and water through these shafts. They are easily eight feet tall and wide. As we delve deeper into the bowels of the city, through varying twists and turns of concrete channels. I wonder how it would feel to be washed away.

As I work with my equipment, placing sensors and plotting an underground mapping system, it becomes more evident that Springer's primary purpose is to eliminate anyone who enters the tunnels. I hope to see no one. But I can't help thinking that it is inevitable, someone is going to breach the tunnels, someone is going to die.

I eventually make it to the end of one of the pipes. Based on the holographic image of Renascence that I have, I can tell that I am relatively close to the perimeter. I run my hands along the mottled seal, having shed my inner queasiness of all things in a sewer days ago. I feel a depression in the concrete, almost like a seam. I take a deep breath and wave Springer over while also indicating silence. He feels the same anomaly and then lights a match, holding it close to the ridge. It flickers, and we know we have found our first breach. My heart begins to beat rapidly as I imagine someone coming through or perhaps just on the other side, listening. Springer is braver than I and he gets down on one knee and presses against the concrete just below the seam. There is a deep groan as it pushes inward on metal tracks revealing the continuation of the pipe, but nothing else. No living thing, only darkness. I lean my head against the wall and emit a shaky sigh of relief.

"I can't say that I'm sad we didn't find something," I say quietly, my voice echoing softy against the walls of the tunnel.

"I feel the same," Springer says.

I am reminded of his face after the previous assignment. I reach my hand out and touch his shoulder trying to convey my understanding. "Let me finish this up and then let's take a break. I think we've earned it."

He nods and walks a few paces away, eyes trained to the opposite end of the tunnel. I place a sensor, about the size of a coin, along the seam at a point where any movement would trip it, but where it will also remain concealed. It's clear from the metal rails that this has been used to enter the tunnels before though it's impossible to say how long ago someone has passed through. The sensors themselves will do little more than alert the Renascence system of an intruder, but I suppose that's all they need in order to send a slew of Sentinels into the passageway. I feel a heavy layer of guilt descend on my shoulders. If someone dies, the blood is on my hands. Again. It's sickening to contemplate.

A short time later we are sitting on the cold cement, backs against the wall and enjoying a snack of hard biscuits and water.

"Do you think we'll find something or someone?" I turn to him and watch him think it over.

"I'm not sure. On the one hand, I am positive that there has been a breach and that there are people who have been in these tunnels in the past, but on the other hand, I honestly don't see them trying to gain access to the city through these pipes, at least not now." His voice is quiet, though easy to hear in this space. I think about what he said.

"Then why do you think we're here?" I ask and feel a nagging suspicion that he is not telling me something. "Do you know something, Springer?"

I can see him debating what to say and then he slowly shakes his head. "I don't know anything. It's just a feeling, but I'm probably wrong."

"What do you mean?" I ask.

Springer turns to me and says, "I feel like a pawn in a

game I don't really understand. Like I'm being moved around, like *we're* being moved around, from one spot to the next and I don't know who is in control of the game. All I do know is that pawns are expendable."

I don't know what to say, so I keep quiet and mull over his analogy. He's right, of course. We're captives in a game that is being played by a faceless entity, forced to make our moves without knowing the cost or the outcome. I have played chess enough times to know that once all of the pawns have been destroyed, checkmate is not far off.

CHAPTER SIXTEEN

And so the hours and the days progress. I find myself becoming used to the dark and the silence. My work is monotonous which leaves me time to think. Thinking can be dangerous, especially when those thoughts run to the people above, those drones who are oblivious to the goings on under their feet. Part of our assignment is to remain at all times inconspicuous and what I find is that being somewhat unremarkable provides me with the ability to notice things that I may otherwise need to ignore for fear of someone perceiving my stare.

But what I notice is that things are not right, not normal. Beyond the prodigious amount of resources that I noted on my first glimpse of Renascence, there is an underlying unease that I feel flowing through its streets, as though the face of the city masks something ugly.

It is startling when it finally clicks. Springer and I

emerge from a ten-hour day in the sewers to enjoy the last rays of sun as they sink below the horizon. It is as we sit on a bench in the outskirts of the commons that I see it. They are all young. It takes me a while for this to sink in, but once it does I can't understand how I missed it. It is a sea of youthful faces, free of the signs of age and experience. No wrinkles here, nor signs of worry, no thin skin and chapped knuckles. I see no aging bodies stooped with aching backs and gnarled hands.

Looking at the residents themselves, I note that the hair color and skin tones show subtle differences, but overall, they are all so similar, like the drones. They are stocky and muscular, healthy, filled with vitality, not scraping by each day trying to fill a hollow stomach. As Springer and I get up and unobtrusively pass through the city, I let my eyes wander discretely noting the details that are so glaringly apparent now. There seem to be a relatively equal number of men and women with a rather prodigious number of children, in fact when I really begin to focus on the youngest souls, I find that their population seems to exceed those of the adults. Clearly, the one child policy does not apply here. It's just another inequity to add to the list. In terms of how they behave, there is little difference from the many kids I knew at home. The energy and squeals of laughter seem normal to me, but that is where the similarity ends. The children of Renascence possess physical traits that are too similar, too specific.

What kind of place is this? My mind spins with possibilities as it becomes glaringly apparent that Renascence is some sort of façade.

It has become more challenging to go below ground, the stillness and gloom no longer comfortable. Each time we do lately, I feel like the dark is closing in on me. I have never been susceptible to claustrophobia but this is pushing my limits so far that I can feel it setting in. It makes me anxious and weepy. I am finding myself wiping my eyes of tears that stem from nothing but the darkness and the grueling hours. I don't know how much more I can take.

The relentless hours in the tunnels have crossed into countless days when I find myself in a new pipeline that resides under the city center. I find more dips and curves than prior tunnels as we make our way through the darkness. I am standing under yet another manhole when I notice that under my feet is a circular opening, sealed shut with a type of wheel on the hatch. I take a step back and motion to Springer, who shines the flashlight on the hatch then looks at me questioningly. Being directly under the medical center in the heart of Renascence makes us cautious and while I want to know what lies beyond the hatch, I am wary of creating too much noise that could lead to our discovery, as we have been tasked to be inconspicuous.

Springer motions for me to step to the opposite side of

the hatch and we lower ourselves onto our knees. Hands on both sides of the wheel apparatus, Springer mouths a countdown from three and then we attempt to turn the wheel. Our first efforts are for naught. The wheel feels immovable, as though it has been sealed by years of neglect but then a low groan escapes the inner gears and we feel it slowly turn. Sweat pops out on my forehead and my arms begin to shake with exertion as we turn the wheel by steady degrees until it finally releases its hold with a rusty sigh.

Springer pulls the hatch open and we are assailed by a pungent stench. I cover my nose while he shines the light into what appears to be a large room, though the depth makes it impossible to see if the space is truly enclosed or is simply another access point to more pipelines. As he slowly runs the flashlight through the darkness, I can see a short ladder leading from the hatch to a metal landing which I assume extends to another ladder to the base of the chamber. The space is unlike anything we have seen up to this point and as my eyes lock onto his, I know we are both wondering if we have found the heart of the breach and the purpose for the system hack.

I am the first to descend. As I step into the room I am enveloped in darkness and a musty smell that fills my nostrils and makes me gag. *Ugh,* I think to myself. *Am I about to step into a nest of rats?* I imagine that I can hear squeaking and the scraping of tiny nails against the cement. But, in the end, I see no evidence of little furry creatures scurrying about and I continue on. As I assumed, the landing does lead to another, longer ladder and I make my way to it. The climb to the floor of the room takes me longer than I had anticipated. The beam from Springer's flashlight is too weak to penetrate the darkness.

Panic sets in as I am enveloped in smothering blackness. My brain conjures thoughts of the roof caving in, leaving me trapped in the dark, buried under layers of rock. I have to force myself to breathe evenly and spend a couple of minutes talking myself out of a full-blown panic attack. I'm getting worse, these episodes are becoming more frequent and debilitating. When I have reigned in some control, I try to take stock of my surroundings. The room has a depth that is completely unexpected and I wonder at its purpose in the past.

Springer is on the landing and making his way to the ladder when my foot slips and I find myself falling. I yelp in fright but hit the ground with a crunch much sooner than I had expected.

Springer's panicked whisper bounces off the walls. "Enora? Enora? Are you okay?"

It takes me a moment to start breathing again and answer him. "Yeah," I whisper back. "I didn't fall too far."

I put my hands out to lift myself up and then jerk them back in surprise and momentary fright. I'm not sitting on a floor, or rather I am on the floor, but the floor is covered in something and it is that *something* that has broken my fall. I feel my heart racing and my breathing takes on a panicked panting. I fumble for the mapping device that slipped from my hand as I fell, cringing as I encounter God-knows-what in my attempt to grasp the familiar object. I am to the point of hyperventilating when my fingers find it, and with a sob of relief I switch it on and the dim illumination pushes back the darkness. As my eyes wander from the glow around the device to the surface below the feeble light, I have to bite the inside of my cheek to keep myself from releasing a horrified scream.

*Oh god...oh god...oh god...*I can't move! *I'm not seeing this*, I tell myself. *It's just a nightmare. Wake up, Enora!*

It's a tomb. This entire room is a tomb!

When Springer's hand touches my shoulder my heart nearly leaps from my chest. If his other hand hadn't covered my mouth, my scream would have reverberated throughout the room and beyond.

"Enora, it's me," he whispers harshly. His hand remains clamped over my mouth. "Don't scream." All I can do is nod as he releases me.

Springer helps me to my feet and I find myself standing on a mountain of bones. I hear a sickening crunch as I shift my weight and a whimper of abhorrence escapes my lips.

They're babies, all of them, the charred remains of their tiny skulls and bones littering the floor in layers upon layers.

This can't be real, I tell myself, but the truth is irrefutable.

Springer is silent as he scans the awfulness buried beneath the city. What does it mean? What would cause so many babies to die and why would they be entombed in this place, this mass grave? The idea of an insidious virus floats through my mind. This would not be unheard of as viral outbreaks are a very real problem around the world. But I quickly discard this idea. I have never heard of an outbreak that targeted only a select group of people, which makes me circle back to the knowledge that this is no accident. I can feel myself shaking, cold to the marrow of my bones.

Springer's voice is startling in the deathly silence when he chokes out, "Let's get out of here."

I don't recall ascending the ladder, nor stumbling through the maze of pipelines. Springer must have dragged me along behind him because I suddenly find myself sprawled on the floor of a tunnel, just beyond the access point we had used in the morning. My mind is fuzzy. I feel myself trying to shut out what I saw, deny the images that are burned into my brain. But I can't.

The Company killed them, hundreds of them. Are there other tombs like this one, hidden under the city in a maze of tunnels? I don't want to be here anymore. I rub my palms against my eyes and feel a gritty substance leave smudges on my cheeks. I jerk my hands away and begin to frantically wipe them on my pants, desperate to get the grit of bones off, but I can't seem to wipe it clean and feel myself slam my back against the passageway in a desperate attempt to get away from it.

Springer pulls himself out of his trance and crouches down in front of me to grab my hands and keep me still. It takes me a minute to register his presence but then I stop fighting and look into his eyes in the shadowy darkness.

"What does it mean?" I whisper.

His head turns to the side, staring off into nothing. "I don't know."

I'm not sure how long we have been sitting. I only know it has been an extended time, as my muscles have begun to cramp and my feet, tucked under me, have long since gone numb. I'm not sure if Springer is sleeping, so I gently nudge him with my elbow, unable to remain in the darkness any longer. He turns bleary eyes to me, nods and slowly rises with a groan from aching muscles. I stagger as I haul myself up, using the wall of the tunnel as leverage. The sensation of pins and needles assaults my legs as I get the blood flowing not only through my limbs but also my foggy mind.

We exit the pipeline and furtively make our way back to the headquarters, closing the door to our room with overcautious silence. I immediately grab a clean uniform and make my way to the showers. As the spray of water washes over me, I see trails of ashes swirling toward the drain to disappear into the bowels of the city, like all of those bodies. As I exit the warmth of the shower and towel myself off, I imagine that I can still feel the fragments of bone under my fingertips and the grit covering my cheeks, it is grime that I can't wash away as this awful knowledge is not something I can erase.

It is not safe to talk here and so we lie in our separate beds in darkness, each with our own terrible thoughts, wrestling our own nightmares, and shying away from uncovering the truth.

I TRY TO DRAG MYSELF FROM A HAZE OF AWFUL dreams when morning comes. Although I am eager to leave the nightmares behind me, they are like sticky webs that snare my consciousness and plague me with images I desperately want to forget. It is the muted sounds of Springer moving about that finally allows me to pull free of the torment and force my eyes open into the light of a new day. I lie in my bed, reluctant to get up and face the task ahead of me. Just the thought of heading underground causes my heart to begin racing. I need to pull myself together but all I see is the tomb, and myself trapped in it.

Unable to delay any longer, I force myself to get up. My hands shake a little as I grab my clothes but I am able to shake off the tremors and finish getting ready. Springer and I murmur a greeting to each other when I emerge from my room and choke down a few bites of food before leaving for the tunnels, the only place that we will be able to break our silence. I force my mind to focus on this as we walk, so I don't feed my growing anxiety.

As we make our way, I view the populace around us. Their likenesses are not an aberration. There is no mistaking the intentionality of the physical uniformity, but the purpose behind it remains obscured. All around me are muscular Sentinels, capped with blond hair of varying shades. Those eyes that I do note, are either blue or green, I don't look too closely though. The civilians are different but equally similar to each other. It's a bit like looking at a group of people all churned out by some factory. We soon pass through this façade and into the depths under Renascence.

Once darkness envelops us, I breathe a sigh of relief at having avoided the claustrophobic feelings of late and lower myself to the hard, cold surface. Springer joins me, and we sit in silence for a time, mulling over what to say.

My voice invades the quiet first. "That tomb had only one purpose."

"Yes, so it appears, but why was it needed in the first place?"

I shake my head, unable to formulate a rationale that would explain the intentional disposal of those tiny souls.

"It makes no sense. I mean, why? You know? Why would they just...?" I can't utter the words. They are too profane.

"Do you think they were all children?" His voice cracks.

"No," I sigh. "Not children. Babies."

Springer turns his head, blindly gazing into the darkness beyond the glow of the flashlight. "This place is not what it seems."

I have been waiting for him to speak my thoughts about what I have noticed since we first arrived. "I know."

"So, care to clue me into what you've already worked out?"

My shoulders sag in relief. I have wanted to share my suspicions but was reluctant to, though I'm not sure why. I spend the next few minutes sharing all of the things I've noted as we've lurked in the shadows of the city. Springer listens, never interrupting, only nodding now and then as if to confirm that he too had noted the same anomaly. By the time I've purged myself of all of my misgivings, I feel drained.

"I guess I haven't really looked at things the way you do." Springer's voice is soft. "Or maybe I just haven't wanted to see, you know?"

I nod. "So, can you make any sense out of any of it?"

I'm so hopeful that as he's listened to my observations he has been able to puzzle out what seems to be right in front of me and yet miles away.

He takes a breath as if to start talking, then pauses before saying, "I think that there are multiple things going on here. You mentioned that the Sentinels show similar traits to each other but you also implied that those traits are not like the civilians. Is that right?"

"Yeah, I see what you're saying. Maybe they have been messing with different growth stimulators or something because the Sentinels are like no one I know back home. These people are like some strange carbon copy of each other, all blond and beefy." As I think on that I realize that's not entirely true. The kids I call drones are remarkably similar.

"Hmm, growth stimulation makes a lot of sense. I mean those guys are big as hell."

"Still doesn't explain everyone else though," I mumble because that's the piece that I find most perplexing and disturbing.

As I concentrate on the many civilians I've seen in Renascence, I begin to catalogue their characteristics. Compiling information is a skill that's become so ingrained in my daily routine that it seems like second nature to apply it to this new conundrum. That they are young was established early on in my observations, but I now realize other blatant characteristics that I previously ignored.

"Have you noticed that the majority of the civilians are probably my height or smaller? I mean, even the men are relatively short from what I've seen."

Springer grunts as he mulls that over. "I guess they do seem rather small. But I wouldn't call them skinny. It's like their bodies are kind of compact or something."

My brows wrinkle as I try to picture what he means. "Huh." I say before adding, "So, what do you think it is that makes them different?"

He shrugs. "I can't say, Enora. It's like pieces of a puzzle that don't fit together."

"Maybe we just haven't found enough pieces yet." I grumble.

He chuckles before adding, "I, for one, am going to get a better look when we head back."

"Me too."

Springer nods and we slowly get up and wander through the dark tunnels until we find where we left off. I'm so eager to get this assignment done. This place isn't natural, and I just want to get out of here.

As we leave this subterranean world later in the day, a feeling of paranoia is prominent in my mind. A crawling sensation is radiating up my spine as though my progress is being tracked by multiple eyes despite how unobtrusive I am trying to be. Do they know what we found? Are they tracking us? I keep my head lowered, as usual, and furtively look around, hyper focusing on the inhabitants that are going about their lives in this cancerous utopia.

As my eyes dart from one individual to another, I layer my observations with that of Springer and see that the civilians do appear 'compact', as he put it. They are somewhat small and muscular but not in the way the Sentinels are, with bulging muscles, rather they have a sort of lean muscular structure that makes them appear strong without the typical physiological features of strength. As we near headquarters, I take one last look and confirm what I had observed early on regarding age and height before we head inside.

I can't share my impressions with Springer, not in this

place of constant surveillance, so I tuck them away knowing they will be in the forefront of my mind as I lay in my bed. We eat a sparse dinner, neither of us feeling much of an appetite before heading to our quarters for a respite for the night.

CHAPTER SEVENTEEN

The next day I head underground with renewed purpose. A restless sleep filled with nightmare images and omniscient eyes has left me feeling frayed and angry and I train this anger to a singular intent: justice. Retribution for what I have been shaped into, for what has been secreted here with utmost care, for the other souls living a nightmare of desperation outside these walls. I feel it burn in the pit of my stomach as I recall the dank pit filled with bones, the strangeness of the people, the brute strength of the Sentinels, and the image of Bram, harbinger of all of this rage.

The fury that I feel gives me strength and a purpose that I never thought to have since learning of my fate as a member of the company. I don't tell Springer about my plans, though I know he can feel my frenetic urgency. It's not that I don't trust him, but if he knows what I plan to do then I am sealing his fate once I am caught. Because I know I will be caught. It is inevitable. But I have accepted this and embraced my single-minded pursuit of the truth.

And so, I re-enter the tunnels under the guise of wanting to simply fulfill our assignment. I ruthlessly shut down Springer's attempts at conversation, and continue to meticulously map each section, paying closest attention to the areas surrounding the tomb. As is our habit, I am often branching off into a previously mapped pipeline to install surveillance equipment while Springer monitors various entry points to ensure our anonymity. It is easy for me to penetrate the building at the epicenter of the city and install apparatus, undetectable to the untrained eye, that will give me access into the one place that I sense holds the key to the hundreds of souls buried under my feet.

Once each device has been installed, I find a section to hole up in and retrieve the data from each instrument creating a holographic image of the lower level of the building. With this representation, I am able to divine an inconspicuous access point into the lower portion of the structure and from this point, I find myself looking at an image of a series of rooms on the basement level that I am hoping will unlock the mystery of the tomb. From my schematic, I can see that there are a couple of rooms that appear to house computers or files of some kind. It is these spaces that I will target.

Next, I hack into the security and surveillance systems. As I am looking over various files, I note that there is an added layer of security that I have never seen before. It appears that only those with advanced levels of authorization have access to this part of the building. This discovery makes me feel certain that there must be sensitive information housed there. From the data I am viewing, the building shuts down from twelve to five in the morning and enters a remote surveillance mode. Using my most recent training, I create a loop in the security feed that I will use to hide my activities when I return to ensure that I am undetected.

Now that everything is in place, I take a circuitous route back to Springer.

As we finish up our rounds, I realize that we are becoming very close to completing our assignment. It takes me off guard for a moment, but then I take a calming breath, comfortable in the knowledge that enough time still remains for me to find what I hope to find and reveal the truth.

Before I can head out of the tunnel, Springer grabs my arm and spins me around. "What the hell is wrong with you, Enora? You've been avoiding me all day."

I knew he'd likely force a confrontation over my behavior and am thankful that it is at the end of the day, that everything is in place.

I pull my arm away and manufacture some tears before crying out, "I need to get out of this place, Springer! I can't do this anymore," a phony sob punctuates my plea as I continue my performance. "I can't sleep without thinking of it and my stomach churns when I try to eat. I need to get this job done...I...I don't even care what's going on here!" I fling my arm to indicate all of Renascence. "This whole place is a fucking tomb!"

I see the skepticism scrawl across his face. I can see his indecisiveness and then watch his face as he capitulates. "Then let's get this job done and get the hell out of this place."

I nod, ashamed of my deceit but confident in its necessity. "Thank you."

Springer sighs, but he doesn't push me anymore and we head back to headquarters, silent and thoughtful.

Keeping a constant eye on the clock, it feels like the numbers are barely moving, but eventually I hear soft snores from the other chamber. I stealthily climb from my bed and make my way out of the room. As soon as I enter the hall, I yawn and stretch for the benefit of the hidden cameras that I know must be watching me at this late hour. Thankfully, I also know that my cover allows me a certain level of protection from any inquisition, especially after our initial contact when we first arrived. I calmly exit the building, an air of importance and surety in my step as I make my way to the subterranean levels of the city. Once there, I can't help feeling a sense of relief and my shoulders sag briefly before I take out my flashlight and make my way to the heart of Renascence.

I should have known Springer wouldn't be fooled. He knows me too well and probably woke the moment my foot touched the floor as I stealthily climbed from my bed. But it startles me when I feel his breath on my neck, as I begin to climb a short ladder to a manhole that opens to a utility room in the basement of the building I am infiltrating.

"Did you really think you could do this without me?" His whisper, barely audible in my ear, startles me so badly that I yelp.

"You scared the crap out of me!" I allow a soft sigh of defeat to escape before slowly shaking my head, accepting the knowledge that deep down I knew there was no way I could do this alone.

"Sorry." But I can tell from his smirk that he isn't.

I turn and look at him. "Together?" He nods, and we enter the building.

It is almost two in the morning as we climb into a utility room, a large space with typical building equipment. I pull up my holograph to orient myself. As an extra precaution, I pull up the identity scans from earlier in the evening and am relieved to see that no one has reentered this part of the building during its nightly shut down.

This is it. I upload my surveillance loop and disable the security and we begin our ascent into the lower rooms of the building. Walking quickly and quietly, we make our way through the rooms to the location that I sense will have our answers.

We find a room with a sign stating records. I close the door, turn on the light, and let out a breath that I hadn't realized I was holding. This is it. Before us are three walls of filing cabinets and then a large, central computer. I am fearful of accessing the computer, but feel it is safe enough to open the files. I motion to Springer to take one side of the room as I head to the wall on the right. My hand is trembling slightly as I reach for the first drawer labeled G1 and noiselessly slide it open.

It is hard to decipher what I am looking at as I scan what appear to be medical records. There is a photograph of an infant with a corresponding identification number: 0001. His grotesquely malformed face is scrunched in a grimace as though he is about to let out a cry of outrage. I trace the image with my finger as though I can reach out and alter the past. I flip to the next page and see a collection of data that is a confusing jumble. I sit down on the floor and read through it, trying to decipher the meaning. After what seems like an eternity staring at and rereading the data, I set the folder aside and reach for another. It is the same: a tiny image of deformity, a corresponding number, a mess of data that I am unable to construe.

File after file it is the same and I soon find that I have come to the end of the drawer. I stare around the room in a daze, each wall is covered with filing cabinets, and each cabinet is filled with images I can barely stand to look at, let alone comprehend.

It is as I'm contemplating the enormity of what we

have found that I finally stop and look at Springer. His face is ghastly white as he pours over the open file in his hand. I walk quietly toward him, almost afraid to ask him what he's found.

He looks up as I step next to him, asking me, "Do you know what this means?"

I shake my head, frustrated that I cannot seem to unlock what should be so glaringly apparent. He turns the folder toward me so that I am looking at the same heap of data that I had seen in each file but was unable to comprehend.

"It's genetic information," he explains when he sees my confusion. "I'm not positive but I think that all of these babies are part of some genetic testing."

"Genetic testing?" I ask, completely at a loss as to why they would genetically test on babies.

"Yes, I think that each of these infants is a kind of genetic anomaly, created in a lab."

I take the folder in my hand, staring at it as if the secrets hidden within the data will somehow fit together like the pieces of a puzzle. But I can't see it. I was never very good at science, didn't really pay enough attention if I'm honest with myself. Now I wish I had.

I wander back over to the first folder that remains open on the floor, subject 0001. I sit down and slowly page through the information when my eyes fall onto something I hadn't seen in my first perusal. Next to the date of birth are two time stamps. Why would there be two time stamps? My brain circles this as I stare at the digits and then it clicks, and a sickening realization sinks into my mind: time of birth and time of death. There is no change in date because they hadn't let him live even one day.

The taste of bile coats my tongue as I lean my head against the wall, dizzy with the knowledge I have found and sickened by what it means. I hear Springer crouch next to me. He doesn't say anything, just gently takes the folder from my open hand and looks at the page.

Through a blur of tears, I manage to utter, "The time stamps."

He grunts as if he already knows. I hear him close and the replace the folder before wordlessly shutting the cabinet. I crane my neck to look at him and take the hand he offers to pull me to my feet. His hand is on the knob of the door when we hear a noise from one of the adjoining rooms and we freeze. We are not alone.

Imprisoned
In an invisible cage
Voiceless misery
Is trapped beneath a façade
The whir of machines
The drip of fluids
Forcing life in a life
While the giver screams
In silence

CHAPTER EIGHTEEN

Springer and I stand motionless, ears pressed to the door as we listen to an inhuman sound echo through the stillness. It is like a low groan, almost a wail in its intensity until it tapers off into silence. Goose bumps cover my arms as I wonder what to do. We wait, breathing shallowly in an effort to remain undetected. Minutes pass with no sound and still we wait. I feel my neck ache with tension as I fight to keep my body still.

Springer breaks the silence. "I think it's gone, whatever it was." But I'm not so sure. I heard no footsteps, just silence after that dreadful noise.

Springer slowly turns the handle and pushes open the door. We see nothing as we enter the hall, closing off the room behind us. Tiptoeing through the dim light omitted by emergency lights fixed along the floorboards, we make our way toward our entrance point. I am almost to the stairwell that leads to the utility room when the hair on the back of my neck stands on end and my feet become rooted to the floor. Beyond the thin wall I'm standing next to, I hear it again, that guttural moan, only now it is more distinct, and I realize the noise may be human.

I feel Springer nudge me forward, but I refuse to move, shaking my head to let him know I will go no farther. Not until I see it. I need to know. I turn to him and mouth the word, *no*, then point to the door beyond which the sound is emanating. He is shaking his head, tapping at his wrist to indicate that we are running out of time. He forcefully tries to turn me toward the stairwell, but I push against him, almost knocking him off balance.

"I have to see this," I hiss. "You have to let me go."

I can see him fight an inner battle and watch as he realizes that I will not be swayed.

"Then I'm going with you," he whispers in the dimness. I nod, and together we walk to the door and slowly enter.

It is like the infirmary at the training center, only there are more machines whirring and beeping softly. Among the machines, at precise intervals, are beds, each one occupied. It is from one of these beds that the sound radiates.

I find myself unable to keep from moving toward the bed, from looking down at the swollen figure strapped to the mattress. It is a woman, only not a woman, for what I see lying there is not a whole person, the eyes are sightless, the pupils and irises covered in a white film. There are no legs, only half-grown stumps, fidgeting restlessly under a thin sheet and blanket. Her arms are bound with her upper torso, anchored to the bed with black straps covered in a soft cloth.

But it is her distended abdomen that holds my eyes and will not release them. I stand there in abject horror looking at a mother, who is not a mother; she is some awful aberration, a breeding machine, no longer human in the true sense. I want to tear my eyes away but I can't seem to make them move as the bloated belly begins to undulate with the movement of whatever is growing inside.

"Oh my God," I utter in disbelief.

Springer forcefully grabs me and hauls me away from the bed, out the door and into the stairwell. It feels surreal as I take hold of the equipment Springer shoves into my hands and robotically reactivate the systems I had disabled. When he is sure that it is safe, he pulls me along and into the darkness.

The shock of what I saw has undone me. Once out of the building and safely in the tunnels, we collapse to the floor, each lost in our own maze of confusion and disbelief. Images flash through my skull, Springer hadn't pulled me away before I could see the rows and rows of beds, all housing a similar mutation, and for a moment I imagine those horrible, cloudy eyes going clear and looking at me in accusation. I bite the inside of my cheek and rock slowly back and forth as I wrestle with the urge to scream.

Springer breaks the silence first, his voice jolting me

from my appalling thoughts. "We need to leave this place, Enora. What we've done tonight, what we've found..." His voice drifts off.

"I know," I manage to croak, though I don't know how we can leave. Our work is not finished and if we were to leave abruptly it would cause undue notice. But I know that I have endangered us with this act and I'm at a loss as to how to fix it.

"What's going on in this place?" I ask him desperately.

"I don't know. They're breeding something, but I just can't figure out what. Those babies looked like some monstrous creation, though I can't imagine that outcome is what was intended. Something buried in their genes wasn't right, something didn't turn out the way they had designed."

I nod. "Those poor women. They aren't even women, not really. They're just...just..." I cover my face, wishing I could cleanse my brain of their bloated bodies. "How many babies have they given birth to? Do you think they are even aware of anything?"

"For their sake, I hope not. Come on, we need to get back." Springer reaches down and pulls me to my feet. The warmth of his hand is calming, and I am reluctant to let him go as we make our way through the tunnel and out into Renascence. When we emerge, I see the landscape for what it is. The fountains and groomed grass are now just a grotesque veneer, no longer beautiful and opulent.

. . .

Somehow I am able to sleep fitfully for a couple of hours, before the sounds of morning wake me. Springer and I eat little, speaking only briefly between mouthfuls of food that seem to stick in my throat, afraid to say too much. I am lost in a maze of horrifying memories and paranoia, fearful that at any moment a team of Sweepers will burst through the door and gun us down. But they don't come looking for us and the fear just sits there in my mind.

We descend underground and head toward an offshoot far from the city center, a place where we feel some measure of safety, find a relatively comfortable outcropping of stone and sit. Our time in the darkness is coming to an end, only a small portion of the sewers left to map. I cross my legs, resting my elbows on my knees and look at him.

"Have you had any ideas that explain what we found?" I ask, hoping his noticeably stronger science background would lend him greater insight.

He takes a deep breath and exhales slowly. "Obviously it has something to do with a genetic trait, like maybe they are engineering some kind of super-human."

"Yeah, like a drone."

"Exactly. The physical characteristics are too common to be coincidence, so that means they are purposeful. While I can understand engineering an elite military force, I can't put together why they would want to create this civilian population."

I think over what he's said. Rows of files flash through my mind, so many attempts with so many casualties. If the Sentinels of Renascence were a successful mutation then why move onto these other modifications?

Close to an hour passes as we continue to toss around ideas but in the end nothing reveals the answer. I half-heartedly get up and follow Springer as he leads us to one of the last portions of the tunnels that I have yet to map. It is back to work for me. At least it is safe, and the relative solitude enables me to continue to ponder the enigma of the women and the babies.

We finally find ourselves at the end of our assignment, but no closer to understanding what we have discovered. Springer seems on edge each day, looking over his shoulder, coiled with nervous tension. To my surprise, I find that I don't feel the stress. It's like I know that if they had discovered our breach they would have already eliminated us, they don't waste time getting a job done.

During our noon break, I plop down onto the floor of the tunnel next to Springer, so close that my arm brushes against his. I feel his muscles spasm at the contact and wonder about it for a moment before I break the silence. "They would have killed us by now if they knew, you know?"

Springer leans back against the cool cement wall. "Yeah. I know you're right, I just can't help this feeling like we're being watched. It's almost like maybe they know what we did and are just waiting to see if we do anything with it."

I nod, though in truth I hadn't considered that they might want to see if we were in league with the rebels or something. But at the same time, I know in my gut that this secret is so big that it would be too risky for anyone outside of the inner circle of Renascence to know about it.

"I hear you, Springer, but do you really think they would let us set foot outside these tunnels with that kind of knowledge?"

I see him consider it before he turns to me. "I see your point. We could have already done a lot of damage with that information. I guess I'm just being paranoid. It's just that I can't stop thinking about it. Those babies. Those women. It's horrible."

I can only nod. It is horrible. "Have you figured out what it all means yet?"

I'm so hopeful that he will tell me he has and that he's just been keeping it from me to keep me safe, but then I see his brows furrow and watch him shake his head.

"I can't see it. They are making something, but I just don't understand what's behind it all."

He looks defeated as he tells me. I feel like we are close to understanding something momentous but are just not able to conceptualize it. In the end we have no choice but to continue on, but it's always there. I can't let it go.

CHAPTER NINETEEN

Almost all of the equipment is in place and the intricate pipelines have been mapped. Only two other breaches have been found during our search, but like the first one, they have long since been abandoned. I begin to wonder at this assignment. It seems strange that we were sent here and given access to a part of the city that ended up revealing secrets I can't imagine the Company would want us to know. I have voiced my skepticism to Springer, but he brushes away my concerns as though they are groundless. I feel like he's hiding something, his responses curt and vague. I don't dwell on my misgivings too long though. The mystery of Renascence dominates my thoughts, and my nightmares.

I have found myself waking up drenched in sweat since that night, often being shaken awake by Springer, who has heard me tossing and turning or moaning in my sleep. It's comforting to know that he is there and at times I fall back into a fitful slumber grasping his hand like a lifeline as he sits on the edge of my bed.

As we enter the tunnels for the last time, I reach out for Springer's hand, pulling him to a stop and looking up into his face. There is so much I want to say but I've never been any good at this kind of thing. In fact, if the truth be told, aside from Bram and Safa, I've never really been able to talk about how I feel with anyone. But looking up into Springer's eyes, I feel a wealth of emotions, from friendship to something more profound. Without him by my side I would surely be lost. He reaches out his hand to gently stroke my cheek with his roughened knuckles. The soft scratching of his skin is comforting.

"Thank you, Springer," I whisper, keeping my eyes focused on his shirt, embarrassed by my feelings and unsure how to say what is in my heart. "I can't imagine being here without you."

"Enora, you are so much more than I imagined you would be," he says softly.

I look into his face, wondering what he means, but he doesn't elaborate and I don't pry. I want to hold onto this moment just a little longer, but all too soon the moment passes and I feel his body shift back to the alert man that I know so well. It's time to finish the job.

. . .

That night as I lie in bed, unable to sleep, something in my mind keeps making me circle back to that disfigured creature we found and the files containing the answer to Renascence if only we could interpret it. I sit up quietly in the bed and peek in, at Springer, trying to detect if he is asleep. Checking the time, I feel a measure of relief to note that it is not yet two o'clock in the morning. I should have enough time to get in and out, undetected. After listening to his even breathing, I silently reach for my uniform. I freeze at every huff of air that escapes from Springer's lips and each shift of his body as I stealthily get dressed and gather the equipment I will need to enter the tunnels.

This time, I need to find the answers and I need to do it alone. I just can't put his life at risk again. If I get caught, at least he could say he had no idea of my intent. I choose to ignore the more likely scenario of him being guilty by association.

As before, I disable the system when the hour hits two and make my way into the bowels of the building and then on toward the lower level rooms we had entered. I tiptoe past the room that houses those poor creatures, cringing when I hear a low groan, and make my way to a room I had noticed on our way out of the building during our prior search. I hold my breath as I turn the handle and make my way inside, silently closing the door behind me. The nameplate outside the door read *Renascence* and this is what caught my eye in the periphery where we had exited before.

I flip on the low beam of my flashlight and slowly scan the room. Dominating one wall is a complex chart depicting what appears to be the evolution of a species, much like a family tree. I can see multiple offshoots identified by genetic coding, all of which end with one word: terminated. All but one that is, Aurora, which according to the map has become the foundation for additional genetic variations, many of which are thriving. I walk closer to the map in order to read the small print under the first successful offshoot. Metabolic and thermoregulation trial, Aurora scion: output and input within target range.

I look at it all again, taking the time to read each notation under the various branches of genetic mutations. Output and input calculations are referenced in every offshoot with those that do not fall within a specified range being terminated. There are so many failed attempts, too many for me to wrap my head around. It's like looking at a complex spider web with interconnected mutations all of which were terminated until one proved successful. In the back of my mind, where I force it to stay, is the knowledge that each of these failures was a living thing, a tiny being that ended up getting dumped into the sewers.

Eventually it comes to me and is so obvious that I can't believe I didn't see it: water. It all comes down to water. The mutations they are creating have some way of processing water that makes them more desirable. They are making a new breed of human, one that they feel could better survive this desiccated world. I have found the answer to my question, the answer to Renascence, the truth behind the Company. But what does that mean for the rest of us?

My legs buckle, and I feel myself slowly collapsing onto the cold, linoleum floor. It all seems so hopeless. What am I even doing here? By completing my assignment I have helped to protect this, this deviancy. My head is swimming with the possible ramifications of my discovery and the role I have played in helping to ensure its concealment.

I almost want them to find me, to storm into this room and end this charade that I'm so weary of playing. I feel like a rat in a maze, only there is no cheese at the end to reward me, there is no end and I just keep running.

Springer doesn't wake, as I silently climb into my bed. I lie on my back and stare up at the blank canvas of the ceiling trying to see this future world that Renascence represents. It is clear that the resources of the city are being funneled to support this designer civilization, all at the expense of the pathetic masses outside of these protective walls. It's not fair that we all suffer so that a group of people can play God.

I feel the impotency of my situation and my complicity in all of this. I want to lash out and take control of my life, but then Springer's warnings float through my angry thoughts. I think of my parents and what would happen to them if I don't play my part.

Play my part.

This is not *my* part. All of this was not *my* choice. I shouldn't have to meekly accept what I loathe and follow edicts from some faceless autocrat who is controlling my actions like I'm a deranged marionette. As I lie fuming, I realize that the puppeteer isn't a faceless master. He's someone I know, or used to know. And he has betrayed me. I let the anger build and direct it at the one person who manipulated my path to discovering this awful truth. *Bram.*

Judas,
What does the mirror hold
when your twisted reflection
looks back at you?
Does it masquerade your perfidy
in a guise of innocence?
Or does it reveal
your treacherous face?

CHAPTER TWENTY

Nothing looks the same, I think to myself, as we drive through the streets on our way out of the city. I am quiet but Springer doesn't seem to notice, lost in his own thoughts. Our assignment is complete and now we are returning. Back to the training center, back to the origin of it all, at least for me. A coal of resentment has been smoldering in my heart since my epiphany in Renascence and I can feel its aim, like a dart, fixed on one person, the one who brought me to this place and made me what I am.

I remember Bram when we were younger, hiding out under the dilapidated eves of some abandoned building in town and dreaming of a future. He always listened to me and never laughed at my hopes for a better life, away from all of it, a life where my daily existence wasn't defined by the number of water credits I had.

It was never a romantic relationship, although if I am honest with myself I know that I did harbor feelings for him beyond friendship. Bram was a person I could talk to without any fear of repercussions. He would just listen, adding his own thoughts now and then, so that I felt free to tell him anything, everything. I told him of my fears for the future, how I dreaded the idea of working in the mill like my parents, and so many others, or ending up as some Company goon. Sometimes I would rail at the injustices that I saw, the clear class distinctions between the haves and the have nots, all because some families sold themselves to the Company in exchange for a gun. Not once did I worry that Bram would betray me, we were too much alike.

Bram lost his mom when he was four and his dad was never quite the same after it happened. He was always in charge of himself, almost like he didn't even have a father, at least not one who gave a damn. So it's no surprise that from an early age he was a serious kid who did what needed to be done without complaint. After all, who would have listened anyway?

I distinctly recall the first day we met. I was five and had just started school. He had just turned nine and seemed so big to my young eyes. I guess I wasn't much different than I am now. I didn't talk much, and my teacher must have completely forgotten I was even there as he led the class out of the building at the end of the day to board the shuttle or walk home. Bram found me sitting on the front steps, lost and scared though I was too tough to bawl about it.

I remember looking up at him through a blur of unshed tears, seeing his grubby hand reach out as he asked, "Where do you live? I'll walk you home."

And he did, never offering a bit of sympathy so that in the end, I swallowed my tears, grabbed his hand, and headed home by his side. After that, we often walked together and soon became inseparable.

The last time we really talked was just before he got his summons for recruitment. We were meeting at our usual spot, hidden from view on the hill overlooking our town. It was a few hours after curfew, the safest time for us to meet when we wanted to talk without prying eyes and fear of discovery. Bram had arrived first and was waiting for me with a ratty blanket spread on the ground for us to sit on, he was always thinking of things like that. A smile spread across his face when he saw me reach the top of the rise followed by a nearly inaudible sigh of relief. He was always nervous I would get caught since my route took me past more surveillance areas, but I was careful, creeping along my often-circuitous path to our meeting spot.

I took my seat next to him and spent a couple of minutes looking out over the horizon, delaying the inevitable conversation that I knew he was waiting to broach. Finally, I turned to him, looking into his patient eyes, and said, "You want to get all serious, don't you?"

Bram laughed though it didn't quite reach his eyes. "Nah. Well, maybe a little."

I sighed. "Okay, lay it on me."

"You're a pain in the ass sometimes," he said while nudging me with a shove to my shoulder. "I'm gonna miss you, if I have to go."

"I know." It hurt to think about it. "I'll miss you too." It felt so final to say it, as though the recruitment had already happened. He was preparing me for the likelihood and I now had to face it. Things would be different. He would be a Sentinel, off in some other world and far from me.

"I need to know you'll be okay." This was so Bram, always mothering me.

I rested my head on his shoulder. "You don't need to worry about me." I owed him that much. He shouldn't be stuck in some training facility worrying over his friend left back home, that wouldn't be fair. I had to be strong. It was time to grow up a little and face the truth.

He nodded. "You should bring Safa up here more often. She's such a rebel these days that I bet she'd enjoy breaking some rules."

I rolled my eyes, thinking about the crap she complained about all the time. "Yeah, I'm sure she'd love to stick it to the Company by sneaking out with me."

"Just make sure you two don't take anything too far, okay?"

"Yes, Dad." I couldn't help piling on a whiny tone to razz him, but underneath I got what he was saying.

In an unprecedented show of affection, Bram gathered me under his arms and pressed my cheek to his chest, clumsily stroking my hair with his rough hands. "Hey, maybe I'll get lucky and we're just getting worked up for nothing."

His words were empty though. Luck just didn't work out for people like us. I inhaled his scent, trying to memorize it to keep me company when he left me to attend training. He chuckled softly. "Do I stink?"

I punched him in his side. "No. You think I would stay tucked under your armpit if you smelled rank? You're my best friend but I wouldn't make my nose suffer for it!"

He cocked his head looking at me, plainly waiting for me to explain my true reason. I looked away and mumbled, "I'm just making a memory, for when you're gone." I glanced up at him to gauge his reaction. His eyes looked pained as he took that in and then he looked off into the horizon, not really seeing anything.

Finally, he said, "I guess we'll find out soon enough."

We spent the next hour talking around the subject that was most on our minds, refusing to face the inevitable. Soon enough turned out to be the next day and we were never the same after that.

CHAPTER TWENTY-ONE

When we return to the center, Springer and I unload our gear and await our debriefing with Bram. I feel nervous at the prospect of seeing him, afraid that he will somehow be able to read my face and know what I'm thinking. I pace along the windows, waiting, while Springer fiddles with some of our equipment. After thirty minutes, Bram finally walks in. I stop mid-stride and face him, clamping my hands to fight my tremors and keep them still.

Springer walks over first, always the leader. "Commander Williams."

"Springer, it's good to have you and Enora back." Bram shakes his hand and then extends it to me.

I reluctantly move toward him and grasp it. I ignore the familiarity this time and cut myself off from feelings better left in the past, where they belong. "Sir."

Bram folds his hands behind his back, greetings having been dispensed with. "I received your report. I am sure that this was a grueling assignment and I appreciate the thoroughness of your work. It is essential that we protect the innocent people of Renascence and your efforts help to ensure that." We acknowledge the compliment, but Springer and I don't add anything. "I would like to remind you of the covert nature of your work. This job is classified. You will not discuss the particulars with anyone other than myself."

Springer and I agree and Bram, satisfied, leaves the room. I can't help feeling like Bram's statement was a warning meant for me. A flare of resentment courses through my body. I don't bother to smother it.

An hour later, I head to my barracks for a little down time. I am lying on my bunk when I feel someone nudge me and look over to see Drake. I spring from the bed, so happy to see his handsome face.

"Drake!" I stand up and give him an awkward hug. He surprises me by cupping my face and kissing me softly. I stumble backward, unsure how to react. My fingers touch my bottom lip. It feels tingly. Is this real? I'm not sure if I'm ready for this.

"Sorry." Drake mumbles.

"It's okay. I've just never, you know."

He smiles and tucks his hands in his pockets. "I feel

like I haven't seen you in weeks," he says with feeling. "Wait, it probably has been weeks."

I smile. "Yeah, it's been crazy, and I've been going at this nonstop. So what have you been doing, were you assigned to a unit?"

I see him look away quickly, as if to scan those around us to see if anyone is listening before he says, "Um...yeah, I'm a Sweeper."

"A Sweeper?" I am mildly surprised that his training shifted away from becoming a Pathfinder. As a Sweeper, he could easily be assigned as my partner and I'm not sure how I feel about that.

"Yeah, it's a great team. I have a good Pathfinder to work with. You know her. She's that friend of yours, Lina Sabins. We've been out for a bit of field work but not much action yet." I try not to curl my lip in a sneer when I hear her name. Ever since she ratted me out to Rafe, it's been a sour relationship.

"That's cool." I hesitate for a moment, finding the right words. "You know, Lina can be pretty self-serving. She's not always the nicest person." I want to say more, but I feel like I have to keep most of it back.

Drake huffs. "I hear ya. She can be kind of a bitch. But she's good."

I get it. He's got to play his part too and being given a partner isn't some kind of trial run. Whomever you are placed with is it. So I drop it. "I have an awesome partner too. Maybe one day we'll be able to work together." I don't honestly mean the last bit, but it seems like the correct thing to say.

"Now that we are both in the same unit, maybe we will. We can talk more about it later. I've got to head out." This is code for meeting up at our old spot and I quickly nod in acknowledgement.

"Sure, see you around." He gives me a short wave as he jogs out of the room.

I sit on the bunk a while longer trying to process it all. It is such a relief to see Drake, but at the same time I'm not sure how much I will tell him about what I have seen, and what I have done.

My first instinct is to tell him nothing. I can't help recalling Safa and how someone knew too much, and it ended in Sentinels dragging her from her house, her parents unable to stop them. By telling Drake, or anyone for that matter, there is an element of risk. Not even Springer knows about my second trip and the implications of the diagram I found. At this point, with Bram's warning echoing in my head, I'm just not sure whom I can trust.

Though it has been many weeks since Drake and I stole away in the night, it feels like almost no time has passed as I slink down the hallway trying to look inconspicuous and slip through the door, finding him waiting for me with open arms. It is strange at first. I can't help but wonder if he'll kiss me again. Do I want him to?

It's been so long since we have been alone with each other and so much has happened, but after a few minutes my shoulders relax, and I melt into his chest, thankful to let the physical stress and anxiety go. I used to be able to feel this sense of relief when Bram and I snuck away, back when things were simpler and my worries were fewer. It's good to have a piece of that feeling back now, though it isn't quite the same. It never will be.

Drake is the first to break both our embrace and the silence. "So, tell me what you have been up to."

I haven't really talked to him for weeks. I'm not sure how to begin and I feel cautious about opening up. So I avoid the question, and turn my head to look at him. "How's it going with Lina?" I want him to tell me that she's awful and he hates working with her.

He smiles. "Lina's alright. I mean, it's not like it would be if I was paired with you, but she's not half bad." I must have grimaced because he laughs and adds, "Not what you wanted to hear?"

I roll my eyes. "I wouldn't mind if you said she gets on your nerves or something."

"Well, she can be kind of a know-it-all and I can't help taking her down a notch every now and then."

I give him a big grin. "Excellent. Have they been working you both pretty hard? Any interesting field work?" I'm fishing for information and hoping I'm not too obvious.

"I've gotta tell you, this specialized training is tough!" I see the glimmer of excitement in his eyes. If he's really into all of this, can I trust him?

I decide to just ask, point-blank. "You like it then? You like being a Sweeper? I mean, it doesn't bother you at all?"

"Sure it bothers me, Enora, but what am I going to do? What do *you* do, just refuse to complete your assignment? I don't think so, I mean you're still here so you must be playing along just like me." His voice is rough and urgent and I feel ashamed to have gone on the attack. He's right. Up to this point, I've just gone along too.

"I'm sorry, Drake. I don't mean to go after you like that. It's just hard, you know?"

"Yeah, I know."

He puts his arms around me and we just sit for a while. It's nice, this companionable silence. I don't feel like I need to talk, I can just be. He must feel it too because I sense his body relax further as the minutes tick by. I know that I could use this time to unload all of my anger, but I also know the risks so I set it aside for another day, another time when I can pull it out and look at it.

All too soon we both sense that it is time to head back before we are missed. Drake makes me promise to meet him again the following night as we leave our secret hide-away. It is on my way back to bed that I wrestle again with telling him what I discovered. On a purely selfish level, I'd like to be able to share some of my burden.

As I let this decision circle my brain, an image of Springer creeps into my mind and I begin to feel like telling Drake, or even meeting up with him in secret, is a betrayal. What would Springer say to me if he knew I was talking to Drake or even meeting with him? Would he caution me? And if he did warn me, what would be the root of his concern? I always feel like Springer is keeping pieces of the truth from me, like he doesn't trust me completely. Clearly, I have kept some things from him too. It may be time for us both to come clean.

The next day is spent at a lengthy health examination. I guess I've been in the field too long and they need to be sure that I am fit before I resume my duties. It is a tedious process with blood and urine tests, cardio exercises, and vision and hearing exams. In the end I get the all clear and am permitted to have rare respite for the remainder of the day. While my initial reaction to the prospect of hours of leisure is happiness, I soon discover that being alone with my thoughts is not pleasant. Springer is nowhere to be found and I feel restless without him. I begin to watch the slow progress of the clock. There is a part of me that just doesn't want to be alone. The nightmares come in the day when I'm alone.

After wasting too much time meandering, I mentally slap myself out of my morose stupor and head to my unit, having decided to take advantage of my isolation. I need a quiet place to think, to consider the various outcomes of any decision I make regarding what I know and how I use it. Once in the safety of the room Springer and I have shared since the inception of our partnership, I sit in the center of the floor and let my mind spin through my memories. It is time for me to look at all of the pieces to this puzzle. I need to find the common thread. Once I do, I feel certain I will know my next step.

So I begin at the beginning, which truly was my recruitment. If I look at myself, I recognize that I am not Sentinel material, never have been. And yet, here I am. So, what was it that caught the attention of the DMC?

I consider the various classes that I took and my progress through that work, but I was average, content to be unremarkable. I preferred it that way. There is my performance on the placement exams that indicated my innate abilities, but I never saw the results of any of those tasks and only heard the results from Chad. If my parents had been Sentinels or in some other high-ranking position, then it would be a natural progression to be selected, though not all offspring of people in these ranks are guaranteed recruitment. As far as I know, there was no one that could have put my name forward.

I take that back. There was one person who could've worked behind the scenes to rig my selection. But why would he want to do that? Has Bram been so brainwashed that he is determined to convert me and suck me into this nightmare? It seems so heartless, but could explain why I ended up here instead of some regular Company job in Prineville. The stab of betrayal I feel is quickly smothered in anger, resentment for pulling me away from everything I knew and making me complicit in the workings of an entity that I never wanted to be a part of. Bram had always looked out for me when I was younger, and I admit that perhaps he feels that this path he has set before is the right one.

From my perspective, Bram orchestrating my ascent into his ranks makes sense. When I consider the role I have attained as being conveniently within his scope of authority, it is all the more believable. Regardless of the aptitude I showed when going through my training, he could have arranged my way into his unit. I just made it easier for him by excelling. From the moment I entered this facility, Bram has manipulated my way under his direction and now I am his weapon. I wear the brand of the DMC on the sleeve of every uniform, and on the parts of me that are unseen and deep within my soul.

Bram is the thread that connects the events that led me to this point. That boy I knew is truly gone. There is no reason that he would see this work as my best future if he still had a shred of the person I used to know.

Nonetheless, I have not sold all of my soul. Not yet. There is a part of me he has not corrupted, a part that has seen more than he had planned. I have performed my job as assigned, at least according to the reports Springer and I send. It is those things I did outside of my assignments that I now begin to analyze.

The benevolent face of the DMC hides an ugly truth.

Whatever they are creating in the bowels of Renascence is a secret they are working hard to keep hidden. I can't help feeling like circumstances strangely aligned in just the right way to enable me to make my discovery. Despite Bram's wish for me to be a 'compliant soldier', I have found a chink in the underbelly of this monstrosity and I am going to exploit it.

As Drake shuts the door of the closet later that night, I am filled with nervous energy, having decided he will be the first who knows the truth. From there, I want this knowledge to spread like fire and destroy the Company. I haven't yet decided how this will play out and I know there are risks involved. There is good chance I could find myself in front of a firing squad, that someone will betray me, but who am I if I continue to be an accomplice to this?

I feel like I am standing on a precipice, ready to take a leap that will be my ultimate rejection of this whole compound and all that it represents. But I can't ignore the niggling worry that if I give in to the need, it'll be an irrevocable mistake. In my mind I see Safa's face smashed to the ground, blood and teeth splattering. Is this the outcome I am willing to accept? For myself, yes. I am finished playing the biddable soldier.

I wrestle an inner battle as Drake begins to talk about his partner and how he's been adapting to his role as

Sweeper, even sharing the ugliness that he's seen and been a part of. As his voice sinks into my brain, I can visualize what he has been through and done, as I have been part of similar scenarios.

"I'm not proud of what I've done, but it's what I have to do, you know?" his voice softens just a little when he says this. I hear his unspoken need for empathy.

"I've seen awful things too, Drake. Terrible things that make me hate the Company."

I begin my story as he listens, without judgment. I tell him how we went to Brigford, a decrepit city, and how the populace was so much worse off than what I had expected. I admit that the televised announcements didn't capture the desolation. There just weren't enough people there to riot or cause the mayhem I had been shown growing up. I leave out our purpose for being there, skirting that issue, and focus on the little things that I noticed and how it felt being in such a large city with a strong Company presence.

As I talk, I gauge his verbal reactions, trying to get a sense of how he would respond if I told him more. I feel his chest rising and falling where it rests under my cheek. It is a comforting sensation that gives me a false sense of security. I am on the cusp of telling him about Renascence when Safa's face invades my thoughts. Her image is not battered this time, she is just there. I pause in my telling and live in the moment, seeing her face so clearly. It is as if

I hear her voice inside my head asking, *is it worth the risk to tell the truth?*

With an involuntarily shudder, the words that are on the tip of my tongue are brought to a halt. If she were here, what would she say? I shake my head imperceptibly, knowing the advice she would give me, and knowing she'd be right. So I listen to her, I embrace her memory and accept that this is not the time for honesty.

Drake senses my hesitation and asks, "What did you find down there?"

His question makes me pause. It strikes me as strange that he would assume I found something when all I've talked about, up to this point, is the strangeness of the city. I haven't even alluded to Renascence and yet he seems to be implying that I was working underground. Why would he assume that? A flare of warning flashes across my brain, and then there's Springer's voice in my head again, like some fairy godmother that whispers advice in my ear when I find myself in a fix. I can hear his voice admonishing me for talking to Drake, for even considering telling the truth and thereby putting myself at risk. It's so real that I can even hear his appalled tone at the notion that I would trust anyone but him.

"What did I find down where? What do..." Drake's hand suddenly clamps over my mouth, cutting me off.

I'm about to bite his fingers in childlike protest, when I see him shake his head roughly. Someone is in the hallway. I stop fighting and freeze, straining to hear the soft footfalls. It's as if whoever is there is trying to be inconspicuous. I am still braced against Drake's chest, feeling his heart thundering; when I hear the footsteps draw closer to the door. It's like a death toll as each step comes closer to us until finally they are directly outside the door. My own heart is racing so fast, all I can hear is blood rushing through my veins. *They'll kill us.* It's all I can think. Suddenly it registers that Drake's suffocating embrace has loosened and he's breathing a huge sigh of relief.

I can hear the footsteps receding down the hallway, when he whispers, "I thought we were caught for sure. We had better go back. That was too close."

I nod, unable to speak yet as adrenaline is leaving my body, giving me a woozy feeling in its aftermath. Drake pulls me to my feet. He wraps his arm under my ribs to hold me steady as I pull myself together and stand on my own.

When I finally wrestle control over myself, the hard reality of it all stares me in the face. We could have been caught. My need for a shoulder to lean on could have cost too much, more than I am willing to wager when it's not only me who would be paying. Anything they would do to me I have already imagined ten times over and those imaginings have been real enough for me to cease to dread any confrontation. But I shouldn't drag him down with me. And I know this should be the last time we meet up. I need to do this on my own. It is the only way that I can live with myself if something goes wrong. Besides, I am the only one who knows the depth of the depravity of Renascence and it will be me who tells it to the world.

Drake is oblivious to my thoughts as we stealthily head down the hall. We walk in silence and eventually veer off to our own destinations. I pause and listen to his footsteps before continuing my own.

CHAPTER TWENTY-TWO

It's bizarre to return to the normalcy of my unit and pick up where I left off weeks ago, before Renascence. I feel like I've been through a war. My soul is bruised and battered from the things I've seen and discovered and the decisions I have made. Add to that the stress of the incident with Drake and I am left with a pounding in my temples as I try to concentrate on tasks I've done a hundred times.

Springer is uncharacteristically quiet, like some silent rebuke. The day drags on, and he remains aloof, making me feel increasingly uncomfortable. When it is finally over, I try to dart out of the room, wanting to avoid a confrontation. But Springer has been biding his time and catches up to me.

"Don't run away from me, Enora," he snaps while jerking my arm.

"I'm not running from you, Springer, I'm running from what we know, what we saw, what we're a part of," my hand flings outward encompassing everything I see. "All of this is a part of it, you...me...all of it!"

"Don't you think I know that? What do you think we can do? What can *you* do?"

My shoulders slump. "I don't know yet. I just..." I shake my head, unable to put into words what I want to do with the knowledge I have.

"You think telling Drake is going to make it better?"

My eyes widen. How does he know about Drake? He watches me closely, so accustomed to my thoughts and actions that I need not say a word for him to know exactly what I'm thinking.

"Yeah, I know about Drake and your secret hiding spot. I was tempted to burst through that door last night and end your little tryst." I can see hurt under the layer of anger as he stares me down. "What makes you think you can trust him, Enora?"

I shake my head. "I don't know. I have to trust someone. I've known him from the start. He's the only one in this bunch of drones who's human!"

"Don't you find his relationship with you a little strange?" He's looking down at me from his greater height. "He could hurt you. You can't trust him. You can't trust anyone. How do you even know if you can trust me?"

"I trust *you*." As I say the words a sense of rightness steals over me. "I trust you, Springer, more than anyone."

I see him nod slowly, relief etched in his face. "Then trust me when I tell you to stay away from him. He's not safe and you're putting us both in jeopardy by saying anything to him."

"How did you know where we were meeting or even that we were meeting to begin with? I mean, I was so careful, or at least I thought I was..." I look up at him remembering those muffled footfalls as Drake and I held our breath in the closet. Could it have been Lina again?

"It doesn't matter how I know. What matters is that if I knew, then who else knows?" His voice is pleading now, begging me to see the danger he senses.

"Are you sure though? Drake is different, I mean he's real, you know? He gets me, and he sees the wrong in all of this too." The last part comes out with a tinge of defensive anger.

I stare at him, feeling a flare of resentment that he's trying to keep me away from someone I care about. It doesn't matter that I've decided not to tell Drake anything. I don't like taking orders, no matter who they come from, and this bucking of authority rears its ugly head despite being directed at the one person who has only ever looked out for me.

Springer sighs, as though he's tired of trying to spell it out for me. "Enora, please listen to me," he reaches out and grabs hold of my arms, tilting me at an angle so that I have to crane my neck and look up into his eyes. "He's not your friend. Do you understand me? Do you understand what I'm telling you?"

I jerk my head, shaking it in denial.

"Drake is one of them. He's like a parasite, skillfully and painlessly attaching himself to you so that you forget the danger he poses. So that you drop your defenses and tell him things you shouldn't tell anyone! He's using you, Enora!" He's shaking me in anger as he spits out. "How can you not see that?"

I don't see it. What could he be using me for? I'm nothing special, never have been. Springer's hands drop limply to his sides as he takes a few steps away and turns his back to me. I see his head drop to his chest. "You have to wake up, Enora. You have to accept this...please." He turns to me. "You said you trust me, right?" I nod slowly. "He's using you. You're going to have to decide, Enora. Either you trust me, or you trust him. But you can't trust us both, because one of us is lying to you."

I'm not sure what to think or who to believe and for a moment I feel untethered and lost. Then I turn to Springer. I can look into Springer's face and see his worry and fear and know that it is real. Whether or not Springer's warnings hold any merit becomes irrelevant. He believes them to be true and I believe in him. So there it is.

"Okay," I say quietly as though afraid to shatter the silence with my voice. "No more Drake, I promise."

I see his eyes soften as he lets out a deep breath of

relief. "Thank you, Enora." And we leave it at that. And it's good enough.

It becomes challenging to fulfill my promise as Drake finds me over the next few days, trying to convince me of a safer meeting place. He plies my conscience with desperate wishes to talk to me, to hold me in his arms, to hear about those things I saw that I never got to tell him. And it is this last wish that makes me circle back to Springer. I find myself replaying my last conversation with Drake and the question he posed that had taken me off guard. It was almost leading, like he knew something already or was fishing for information that he suspected I had. I look at his incredibly handsome face and wonder if it hides something. My mind goes back to the time he kissed me. Does Drake *really* like me? Or is Springer right? Is he just using me? I listen to Drake's pleas and my uncertainties grow, little by little.

However, I know that I need to continue the ruse, Springer would expect me to 'play my part' and avoid suspicion, but that is easier said than done. I'm not the greatest at coming up with valid excuses and lies on the spot. I'm more the type to think of great ones long after, as I'm perseverating over it. And so my excuses end up sounding lame. I can see that Drake doesn't believe me but is willing to play the game even if he can't fully hide the irritation simmering below the surface. In the end, I'm forced to play upon any inherent sympathy he might have and simply tell him that the last night really spooked me and I'm just too scared.

"We need to lay low for a while and make sure it's safe," I tell him. "Just a few days, okay? It's just too scary right now," I explain while infusing a slight pleading into my voice.

This seems to appease him. "Maybe you're right. I just can't stop thinking about what else you were about to tell me. I hope you know you can trust me, Enora."

I smile, looking him in the eye and biting my cheek to keep from asking him, point-blank, if he's being honest with me. I manage to dredge up something to say, though it's tinged with falsity. "I do trust you, Drake. And I want to finish what I was telling you. I'd feel so much better if I could get it off my chest." His eyes light up and I'm vaguely impressed with my acting abilities but stifle the urge to give myself too much credit.

"We'll give it a week and if everything seems normal we can meet at the new spot I found. We won't have to share a space with cleaning supplies anymore." He reaches out and brushes a few loose strands of hair away from my face. "You can tell me everything, Enora. Don't you trust me?"

"Of course I do, it's just...I don't know."

His brow furrows. "Has someone been badmouthing me or something? Why are you pushing me away like this?"

"No one has been saying anything! I'm just not good at this, Drake. I don't know how to act. I've always handled things mostly on my own, you know?"

He gives me one of his classic smiles, the one where his dimples show. "Let me help you, Enora. I promise you'll feel like a huge weight is off your shoulders. I care about you. You're beautiful and smart. You're my only real friend in this place. In fact, well, I think you know I'd like to be more than friends. Don't you feel it too?"

I can't deny that I find him incredibly attractive, who wouldn't? No one, ever, has said I was pretty. I've always been the scrawny girl with a plain face. To hear him say I'm beautiful pulls at me in a way that I'm not prepared for. And I guess it's how strange this is that makes me wonder if it's real. I manage to say, "I care about you, too." But, in truth, I don't understand how I feel. The lie, no matter how small it is, tastes like charcoal in my mouth.

Drake gives me a crooked smile. "One week and then you can let this all go. I'll take care of you and you won't have to be alone with these secrets anymore."

He leans forward and gives me a soft kiss on the forehead before walking away. I watch his receding figure, hands clenched at my sides. I feel an inner battle brewing as my eyes stare at the space he left. In my head, I hear Springer's warnings and know that I can't put limits on my faith in him. But it's so hard to accept what he believes. I tell myself that Drake is just using me, but only a small part of me really believes it. So I force myself to repeat it, for Springer's sake. When I've said it enough times, I turn my mind toward the promise of a fitful sleep and await the next day when I can be with the one person I can really trust.

I HAVEN'T EVEN FINISHED WALKING INTO THE ROOM when I curtly ask, "Do we have another assignment yet?"

I can see by Springer's reaction that my tone has surprised him. "You *want* an assignment?"

"We have a job to do."

He nods, understanding without needing me to cough up an explanation. He's been watching my mood steadily deteriorate since he told me about Drake and must know that it's wearing me down.

"There's nothing for us yet, but I can remind Bram that we're ready to go back into the field."

My lip curls in distaste when he says Bram's name and I feel that core of anger that I've been nursing flare up in response. I feel the gears in my mind spinning from Bram to Drake and back again and then the gears stop, locked into place like pieces of a puzzle.

"It's Bram," I whisper.

"Huh? What's Bram, Enora?"

"Drake is a spy for Bram."

I see Springer shaking his head in denial and I cross the room to look him full in the face.

"It all makes sense, Springer. He's behind it all, what I

am and what I've done and now he wants to be sure that his little robot is following orders! He's sent Drake to spy on me and find out if his pet project is spilling her guts!" It feels good to let this anger and resentment course through my veins and, though I shy away from it, it's good to direct the rage away from Drake.

"You're wrong, Enora," Springer quietly interjects.

"No, I'm not. You don't understand. Bram and me... we...you just don't understand," I can't explain it and even if I could, Springer wouldn't accept it in his current state of mind.

I turn my back on him and fix my gaze on the training yards outside the windowpane. I can't understand Springer's refusal to see the truth, but I don't need him to agree with me, I just need to get out of here.

After an awkward silence I say, "It doesn't matter anyway, Springer. It's not like this makes anything different. I still want to go back into the field. I can't...I just can't be here right now. I can't see him every day, knowing that he's not what he seems to be." I let him think I'm talking about Drake, it's easier that way. I turn pleading eyes to him and I can see the fight drain out of his stiff shoulders.

"I'll get us an assignment."

"Thanks."

Warriors are not born
They are made
Their birth
A violent wrenching
Through a soft veil
That conceals
Their brutal heart

CHAPTER TWENTY-THREE

Springer is a man of his word. Bram arrives the next day to give us an outline of our new task. "You will be addressing a situation in our local food production plant. As you are probably aware, these terrorists have no tracers, having been born outside of any community. This means that your surveillance expertise and knowledge of the facility will be of utmost importance. Enora, I would like you to spend the remainder of the day reviewing your technical training, particularly with code. Prior to your departure, I will provide you with security clearances that will enable you to enter the plant's network and determine if the system was hacked."

"Yes, sir." I prefer to learn about the cyber-world lately. It feels removed from the reality of what we are doing.

Bram looks at Springer. "You will need to become acquainted with the entire facility. It is essential that you have familiarity of the structure itself and all operations within. I will give you specifics this afternoon when you collect your identifications."

Springer thanks Bram and we take turns shaking his hand. I have turned my attention away from him, when Bram says, "Enora, I trust that your work will reflect the expertise I have seen in your previous assignments. The successful completion of this job will have its rewards."

It's a strange comment and I'm not sure how to take it. Is he complimenting me? Am I going to receive better housing after I do this job? Is he trying to say he's watching me closely? I hate to think of him manipulating me like a pawn, but there is nothing for it. "I will give it my best effort, Commander."

"See that you do." He adds before walking out.

I have an insane urge to flip him off. He's acting like a Company thug with his subtle warnings and bribes.

I AM THANKFUL WHEN OUR NEW JOB IS FAR REMOVED from the city or any neighboring town. We have been assigned to the largest food processing facility in the state and I'm eager to go for reasons well beyond getting away from Bram or Drake. This opportunity may provide more insight into the workings of the Company and I see this as another weapon at my disposal. As Springer and I pass through the barren landscape, I can't help feeling a sense of freedom. I always have this sensation when I leave the training center, but this time it is more prominent.

The ride is monotonous, and I am able to reflect on my decision to act on what I know. Up to now, I have kept quiet about the information I found on my last trip into the Renascence headquarters. Perhaps I was waiting for this opportunity or maybe I just needed time to sharpen my weapon of knowledge. Whatever the case, I decide that the time is right.

I slightly raise my voice above the din of the jeep. "I need to tell you something."

"Oh?"

"I returned to Renascence headquarters while you slept."

His eyes swing to mine and the jeep swerves slightly. "Are you insane?"

I hold up my hands, halting his words. "Springer, I needed to know. And it's time to tell you what I found. I guess I was waiting to see if I got caught."

"Dammit, Enora!"

"It's okay. I'm okay."

I see him clench his jaw, no doubt grinding his teeth in irritation. He's so righteously angry at the risk I took. I understand that. We've been through so much together and I kept this from him.

"I'm sorry."

He huffs, but I know I'm forgiven. "Tell me then."

I lay it all out for him, the strange evolutionary web, the offshoots that were terminated and those that remained. My own theories as to why these mutations were created. I tell him all of it, leaving nothing out. When I am finished, I feel as though a weight has been lifted from my shoulders. He's quiet so I ask, "So, what do you think it all means? What is the purpose for Renascence?"

Springer takes his time replying. I look out the window, giving him the mental space he needs to analyze everything I've said. "I have a couple of thoughts. I think that there are parallel mutations being generated. Almost like a warrior class and a civilian class. I agree with you that there is a direct relationship to water. It's clear that the Company sees this genetic manipulation as beneficial. My thought is that perhaps they are hoping to eventually cross breed both mutations, thereby creating a human that would have multiple traits that are desirable."

I chime in. "I see where you're going with this, but what is the end game?"

"It could be as simple as designing a breed of human that will become the ruling caste. What if there is some type of mental conditioning in this whole process? Then it follows that these individuals could ultimately be brainwashed." He pauses before adding a final thought. "Imagine what they would do if they had no conscience. Or if they simply believed that the rest of us are expendable. Or maybe they'll just be better suited to survive in this world."

Springer's theory reinforces my need to somehow unmask the face of the DMC. The world needs to know what they are. Perhaps in some way, by uncovering the truth I can find justice for Safa, and for myself.

Having unburdened myself, I exude an air of calm as we speed along the road. He may not want to stand with me as I fight the power that I am determined to bring down, but I feel at peace knowing that he won't stop me either. My admission has brought us closer. For better or worse, we are the keepers of a dangerous secret and, in that, we are united. I feel strong and ready.

Since I was a child, I've wanted to see a food processing facility in person and, prior to this mission, the closest I ever came was that distant view on our way to the city. I have always wondered what it looks like inside and how the Company grows so many crops or raises so many animals. As we get closer to our destination, I am filled with excitement to find the answers to my logistical questions surrounding how the DMC grows, raises, or manufactures the food I have eaten all my life.

I never learned when the Company took over food production, and my parents never spoke of it. So aside from information from texts or teachers, I have very little knowledge of the inner workings of each type of food producing facility. In my imagination I see rows upon rows of lush vegetables, plump tomatoes and crisp lettuces. I can picture trees dripping with sweet fruit and imagine the scent of soft peaches or tart apples, delicacies that I had little opportunity to experience growing up. My stomach rumbles as my thoughts drift in a cornucopia of food. A small smile curves the side of my mouth as I envision a dairy farm with cows devouring grass in an open field or being milked while happily chewing their cud. I know it's a ridiculous vision. The dairy processing plants are likely rather crude, concrete and steel operations. But it's my daydream. I'd much rather think of cows frolicking through a field than in a cold structure far from fresh air and sunlight, never mind that *I've* never even seen a field of lush grass.

As Springer drives, he fills me in on our directive and my excitement begins to wane as it becomes clear that a group of rebels have been infiltrating the facility. We are being tasked to discover their origins and eliminate the problem. I can't help wondering about these people. They must live in perpetual desperation, being separate from everything that allows the rest of us to survive. I wonder what it would be like to join them. The stark landscape flies by while Springer drones on about the specifics and I sit in silence with the realization that there is no escape from this, not yet. I move from one prison to another, though no bars surround me.

A few hours later I see the facility growing in the

distance. It's huge, a monolith of human ingenuity. I feel Springer look my way, smirking at my obvious awe. "Bigger than you expected?"

I face him, trying to contain my shock. "Um, yeah, you could say that. What the heck do they grow in there? Giant, mutant cows?"

Springer laughs. "No, this is just a typical food production plant." He registers my skepticism. "I'm being perfectly honest. Think of it this way, this particular facility feeds Brigford's population plus a smattering of the towns on the outskirts."

I turn my attention back to the building, trying to take it all in. The closer we get, the more I come to recognize those elements that I've learned are a part of every greenhouse run by the Company. Surrounding the facility is typical barbed fencing with the added component of electrical current running through it, as evidence by the warning signs I see posted as we pull up to the checkpoint. And sure enough, there are solar panels and huge windows to maximize use of the daylight. Now that we are closer, I can see that there are many levels of greenhouse and separate buildings that I can only assume contain differing types of plants.

During the commute, Springer had informed me of our cover. We are inspectors doing an assessment of the productivity, security, and procedures of the processing plant, hence the small variations in our uniforms. Like our assignment in Renascence, it's a necessary subterfuge. The guard places a security placard on the jeep's windshield and we head through the gate to a designated area of the lot that houses the central offices.

As usual, I let Springer do the talking. He's so much better at bullshitting than I am. My part is to stand, arms folded, looking mildly irritated. I manage, but I hardly think I pass as some hard-ass.

Once we've been verified, we are led to our temporary housing, which is located on a lower level of the central office and consists of a two-room unit with a small sitting room, eerily similar to our quarters in Renascence.

Our guide, a young man about my age, hands Springer a key card then turns to me. "Are you agents?"

I'm taken off-guard, unfamiliar with the term, but am saved by Springer who quickly replies, "I don't believe that is an appropriate question."

I actually hear the guard's gulp as he realizes that he may have committed some gross error in judgment by effectively asking our business. His face flames, as he stammers, "Of course not sir, my apologies." After which he quickly escapes our vicinity.

Springer chuckles softy. "Damn, I'm good. Hope he didn't piss himself running away from us!"

"You're incorrigible. He's just a kid."

He just grins at me. "Go choose your room, Enora. I'm going to unpack and pull up a map of all known access points so that we can get started first thing."

As I begin to walk away, I turn to him. "You should

also download personnel information so we can cross reference."

Springer winks. "That's my girl."

I smile and head to one of the two bedrooms. It is small and stark, but I sigh in gratitude at having a private place to drop whatever façade I'm forced to wear. The bed beckons so I drop my bag with a clunk and fall face first into a surprisingly soft mattress.

For a few minutes I keep my focus on the scent of the sheets and thin blanket, blocking any thoughts from creeping into my consciousness. I let myself be in the moment, knowing I have a job to do here. One that will likely prove as hard as those I have been a part of before. But I force myself to focus on how I can engineer this experience to my gain. I have been a pawn in someone's game for too long. Springer and I are like the cogs of a wheel on a runaway car. Unable to change direction or stop, as we barrel into an innocent crowd who wants nothing more than to live without the misery that is their only reality. I fall into a deep sleep with visions of Renascence spooling through my head.

A gentle shaking pulls me from disturbing dreams that I can't recall but leave me with an ominous feeling, like poisonous spiders creeping into my skull. My eyes focus on Springer's face, hovering a few inches above my head.

"You were whimpering in your sleep. Want to talk about it?"

My brow creases as I try to capture fleeting images

from my dream, but they dart around escaping me until I cannot recall even the slightest impression. "I can't remember."

Springer searches my face, likely gauging whether or not I am withholding anything from him, but it becomes clear that the haze of sleep is real and my memory is a quagmire of random thoughts. As he continues to sit, I begin to wonder why he isn't leaving and letting me slip back into the arms of unconsciousness. I study his face and note that he looks haggard.

"You weren't sleeping at all, were you?"

He takes a deep breath and slowly exhales. "No, I wasn't. I haven't made out too well in the whole sleep department lately."

I feel badly that I have been so wrapped up in myself that I hadn't noticed the worn look in his face and the dark circles under his eyes. "Do *you* want to talk about it?"

"I'm not really sure what to say," he says quietly. "I find that there is always a part of my mind that is struggling to suppress everything when I'm awake. When sleep finally comes, the ghosts of my actions haunt me. We all have our demons, Enora. Mine just wear a face."

"I see them too." But I know it's not the same. He's protected me from the ugliness. "Maybe we need to be more honest with each other and stop battling these thoughts alone."

Springer nods. "Yeah, maybe that would help."

But he is not forthcoming, and it takes me some time to

realize that he won't want to talk about anything specific here, where we could be monitored even now.

So I yawn to feign exhaustion, paranoia is setting in, and tell him, "I'm beat for tonight so could we talk it out tomorrow?"

His eyes crinkle in understanding and a small smile curves his lips. "Sure, sleepyhead." Springer stands and softly pads to the door, glancing back once to give me a quick wink.

IN THE MORNING WE BEGIN THE FIRST OF MANY rounds through the complexities of the food processing facility. I am in complete awe of the magnitude of the place and begin to wonder why more food wasn't rationed to my family while I grew up. In fact, why didn't all of Prineville see more rations?

Undoubtedly, the most impressive of all is the use of recycled water, so much like Safa's invention though on a much grander scale. Safa. It is at times like this that I feel a deep sadness and guilt that I have left her behind. She would have been such an asset to this place, helping them to improve on their designs. Everyone in my town could've benefited from her creative vision. As an image of her face enters my mind, I wonder if she's even alive, if they killed her, or if she's trapped somewhere in her own private hell as punishment for bucking the system. I wonder who turned her in.

Springer's voice pulls me from my musings. "There have been cyber-breaches mostly, from what the report says, but it's clear that a physical operation is coming and we are tasked with finding out where this group originates from."

Thinking of what must be a ragtag group of survivalists, I can't help asking, "Why are they trying to break into the building? Is it just for food?" In my mind, I wouldn't blame them for trying to steal from this gluttony.

Springer looks at me. "Does it matter?"

I shrug. "I don't know. I mean, what if they're starving?"

Springer grabs my arm and whispers harshly in my ear. "We are here to do a job, not to ask questions." His eyes pointedly roam our surroundings so that I'm reminded of those ears that may be listening too closely. I see a guard a short distance away, eyes averting when my gaze falls on him. I need to be more careful.

What Springer doesn't add in his overview is what we are tasked with once we know their location, but it's there, the ugly reality of the ultimate goal of our assignment. The day wanes and by the end we have been through the entire facility and know where each of the operation hubs is located. After dinner, we can return and get to work.

My preparatory training for this job has focused on the use of various computer programs that allow me to identify and utilize back doors into networks. I find these tasks to be much like a maze, only in the cyber realm, so it is familiar territory as I am, in essence, simply generating a path to infiltrate a system. Combine this training with the access codes that Bram provided me as part of our cover, and it's an easy job to enter the system and begin to search for hacks. It is like my Pathfinder role is growing to include both the physical and cyber world of mapping and I am feeling more comfortable navigating both realms. As Bram indicated prior to our departure, a group of terrorists have been able to infiltrate the system. It is my job to find out what information they accessed and how they plan to use it.

I begin to sift through reams of information and lines of code. Springer is off on his own part of our mission, becoming familiar with the building and analyzing potential access points that could be utilized by rebels. He provides various updates as he runs around the structure, becoming acquainted with the various routes I have mapped and indicating any additional information he needs. It takes some effort to flip back and forth between his needs and my computer work. But after a time he finishes and joins me, easing himself into a chair, exhausted.

Time passes quickly as I become completely absorbed in my task, thankful that my mind is fully engaged in something beyond my own morose thoughts. I'm so focused that I forget that Springer is with me until I hear his deep breathing and look over to see his head resting against his chest as he sits sprawled in the chair. My hands leave the keyboard, as I lean back and watch him sleep. The dark shadows under his lowered lashes are so prominent under the lights as I look at his face.

Poor Springer. I only know what we have been through together but as I gaze at his slumbering form, I wonder what other things he's seen and done that keep him up at night. I feel shame wash over me as I accept my selfishness, so little of my thought has gone to others as I am only too ready to devote all of my attention to my own misery. I shake my head and make a pact with myself that I will be a better friend and take care of him the way he so obviously takes care of me.

I resume my work, content to let him get whatever rest his poor body needs. It is a couple of hours later that my diligence pays off and I find the first breadcrumb. I can see an interrupted line of code, a backdoor into the system. I follow this, and I am able to see what parts of the network were accessed. As I continue to follow a trail of hacks, my fingers pause just above the keys.

If I go down this path, there is only one outcome. These rebels, whoever they are, will be destroyed. Their motives won't matter. A traitor is a traitor. What if this group is just a bunch of kids, youths like the ones Springer killed in Brigford? Do I honestly want to be a part of that? Bram's image enters my mind and with it a burst of anger. For me, his is the face of the DMC. He is the one who put me on this road to discovering whomever is on the other end of this trail. And it is Bram who is ordering their execution should I find out where they are. I'm a marionette. I can feel the strings he's pulling and want to rip them away. I am done being some pawn he can move around like a mindless weapon. I feel my body burn with anger and begin to rise out of my seat, ready to walk away from all of this, to expose the truth. But then I hear the low rumble of Springer's snore and turn toward the sound. Can I do this without taking him down with me? And my parents, what of them if I turn traitor?

I feel air rush out of me, along with my rage, as I watch Springer's even breathing. How could I put him at risk? I sit down with a resigned thump, and refocus my thoughts to the task at hand, following the trail to see where it leads. By being a good soldier and continuing to hide the truth, I will ensure that Springer and my parents are safe. As much as I hate it, I must do this job and all others that follow. I owe them that much, and maybe even more.

A couple of hours into the labyrinth of code, I find what I've been looking for, an IP address and approximate location of origin. It is a strange feeling that washes over me as I unlock this bit of information. I can't help but vacillate in my decision of whether or not to alert Springer. I know the result if I do. *Murderer,* whispers through my mind. It is during this internal battle that Springer leans too far over in his chair and jolts awake.

He rubs his hands over his face in an effort to come

fully conscious. "Sorry about that, Enora. I didn't mean to fall asleep on you." He yawns and stretches. "Find anything?"

I watch him for a moment longer before responding. "Yeah, I did."

CHAPTER TWENTY-FOUR

Once I have identified the backdoor that the rebels have been using, it is a simple thing to monitor the parts of the system they have been targeting. I can then use that to determine how they may breach the facility. I keep Springer updated on what I find and how I think it will be used to gain physical access to the facility. He begins to plan an ambush. It's brutal to see him work through various scenarios as he determines which weaponry to use and what vantage points are best for me.

I am on edge each day as I see more and more rebel activity and know that the time is coming close. It would be such a simple thing to cut off their backdoor and alert them to my presence in the system. But I don't act on this urge. I keep my promise to get the job done.

In the off hours, we wander the facility to learn the ins and outs of each portion of the complex so that we are well versed in how to best use the building itself to counter the forthcoming infiltration. The workers naturally give us plenty of latitude. The uniforms guarantee that and Springer's air of authority just furthers our disguise.

As we go about our business I am in constant shock at how much food is being produced and can't help to compare it to the little we could afford as I grew up. I equally can't help but compare it to how much went into the mouths of the residents of Renascence, or to what I get now that I'm one of the elite. I wonder if they even use water credits. As I ponder that thought, I flip through my memories and realize that I never saw anyone place their arm in a scanner, not even the Sentinels. It's like they have been placed so far above us, some super-elite class that is provided with all they could ever want or need. The rest of us fought like starved dogs for scraps. I feel my hand clench and force myself to release my grip and let out a slow breath to temper my anger.

It is pure luck that I happen to be deep within the system's security when the rebels decide to penetrate the facility. Admittedly, their timing is ideal as the few Sentinels on duty are naturally lax at this hour of night. As I watch the system's outer security measures be turned off in one small section of the compound, I am almost numb with disbelief and feel myself strangely rooted to my chair. A part of my mind flashes a warning, like some premonition that if I alert Springer then I will be setting off an irrevocable chain of events. It is enough to gag my voice and force my body to feel leaden and unable to move. I find that I can only sit and watch the blips on the screen, paralyzed.

Springer's sudden presence at my side is what finally releases me from immobility and I turn to him and whisper, "They're here."

He jumps into action once I've given him the coordinates of the breach. I watch as he grabs his gun with a silencer and stuffs a wicked looking knife into his belt. My heart is starting to race, and I feel that premonition creep back into my mind. Something is going to happen. My brows furrow and I look up at Springer. "Let's not do this."

He turns a startled look at me. "What?"

I get up from the chair. "Something isn't right, I feel it. This is wrong."

He looks at me and calmly says, "We have to do this."

I shake my head in denial. "No." I grab at his arm. "Something bad is going to happen." I can't seem to put into words the dread I sense, and he looks at me with slight annoyance, no doubt concerned about the time we are losing debating this.

"Listen to me." His eyes bore into mine as though they hold some hypnotic power. "This is just another job. I won't let you get hurt. You won't even be near any real danger."

Frustration bubbles over as I snap at him. "I'm not

worried about myself. It's just this whole situation...it's... ugh! Why do we know so little about the people behind this?"

Springer looks at his watch, no doubt reminding me of the time ticking away. "Look, these people could be planning to blow this whole place to hell. We have our orders." He looks away and I know deep down he sees the wrong, but this is not the time to explore it. "I can't do this without you."

I nod in acceptance, but my heart is torn. This isn't right. There has been no effort to hear from the other side. According to the Company, there is no other side, or no argument that could validate traitorous behavior, such as this. I've never been a really intuitive person, but I just feel like Springer and I are taking a step toward something that could change us forever.

"Come on, we need to get into position."

He shoves my equipment into my arms and pulls me out of the door. Presentiment or not, we head out toward the breach.

THEY HAVE COME IN THROUGH AN AIR DUCT THAT HAS an intake vent just inside the perimeter's fencing on the southwest corner of the building. Like the rest of the compound, the fence and duct are fitted with sensors which would have triggered an alarm had the system not been hacked and the security disabled. It is a clever access point, both inconspicuous and easily navigated if the schematics have been downloaded from the network. From the ducts, someone could reach multiple food storage rooms.

I use my infrared equipment and track the progress of five individuals who are making their way into the first level storerooms. I relay my information to Springer and watch as his illuminated figure moves stealthily into position. Our instructions have been to apprehend one rebel for interrogation, a task that I have shied away from preparing myself for. It will likely be up to me to hold this individual while Springer terminates the other four people. I feel squeamish at the thought of this part of the plan, though I know it is a necessary evil if we are to complete our assignment.

The five figures that I am tracking pause above a ceiling vent and I watch as they prepare to enter a storeroom. Springer is just outside the door, waiting for me to input a code that will unlock it so that he can enter the room unnoticed. It is a large space with multiple shelves of food, which will allow Springer to move through the room to each person. I note that one individual remains in the air duct as the others appear to lower themselves into the room. I wait, wanting them to feel secure before unleashing Springer.

I watch them move through the room, grabbing items, which are then pulled up into the vent. They are choosy with what they take, not simply ransacking everything in sight. As the four figures move further into the room, away from the door, I enter a code and watch as Springer opens the door and goes inside. I whisper the location of the targets, afraid that my voice can be heard through his earpiece in this quiet space.

Springer moves down the aisles of shelving, coming closer to one of the figures. I watch in horror as the figure he is targeting suddenly freezes and then runs. I hurriedly tell Springer, who takes after him. But now I see that the other three individuals are heading Springer's way. I'm trying to relay it all as fast as I can over the shouts of alarm coming through the microphone, when I see Springer fall under the weight of a body that has come crashing down on him.

"Springer!" I shout, dropping my equipment and racing to his location.

My feet pound on the hard floor as I storm through the corridor desperate to get to him. All I can think, is that my fears are coming to fruition. I'm going to lose the one person who has kept me from drowning in the darkness of my own mind.

It seems to take me an eternity to get to the storeroom and all my thoughts are focused on the terror I feel at knowing that I'm going to lose him. I'm taken by surprise when my body is flung backward, striking the ground so hard that my breath is completely knocked out of me. I stare up at the ceiling trying to suck air into my lungs and make sense of what just happened when I hear the ragged breathing of someone next to me. I blink as air fills my lungs and I turn my head to see my attacker.

He's struggling to get to his knees, cradling an arm that has clearly been broken when he landed badly on the floor. I notice that his hair is cropped very short to his head and his clothes bear the signs of heavy use, worn and stained. I sit up slowly, realizing that I am completely at his mercy. He makes it to his knees and then looks over at me.

I feel like I have been punched in the gut. He's a child, maybe thirteen. Frightened eyes stare out of a face streaked with tears of pain, his cheeks pale. I watch as though outside of myself as he uses his good arm to pull a knife from his pants and point it at me. I focus on the blade, watching as it wobbles in his shaking hand. His fingers are caked in dirt, dark brown crud lodged under each nail, but I can still make out the white knuckled string of his clenched grip. He's so impossibly young. My eyes shift back to his face and I can see the uncertainty there, along with the innocence and terror. I slowly raise my hands in a gesture that I hope will exude my desire to leave him unharmed. As he watches my movements, I see a look of relief wash over his face as he realizes that I pose no real threat.

The knife begins to lower, then stops midway in the air. I watch as his face tilts downward to stare at his chest where I see a red spot blooming across his filthy shirt. He looks up at me in shock, mouth gaping open and then slumps, face first, to the floor.

"No!" I scream and grab his frail body, turning him over and cradling his head in my lap.

His youthful eyes stare up at me in confusion, unable to grasp what has happened, that he is dying. A sob escapes my throat as I hear rattled breathes gurgling out of his mouth and watch a trail of blood slip through cracked lips, falling onto my leg and soaking into the perfect fabric of my uniform.

I watch his mouth gape open and closed, desperately trying to pull air into lungs that are too damaged to take it. His body spasms in the throes of suffocation, blood filling his lungs. And then the light goes out of his eyes and he's gone. This child is gone, in my arms.

Someone starts screaming as I hold his small body and the sound is getting louder and louder until it is deafening. I feel an ache in my throat and realize it is my own voice echoing around me. But I can't stop screaming and my voice goes hoarse until all that comes out are broken shouts and fits of coughing. I can't tear my eyes away from the boy's face, from his frozen gaze. Not even when the guard, who is suddenly there, shakes me roughly while yelling at me to stop screaming. It is only after powerful arms wrap around me that I pull my eyes away and come face to face with Springer.

I let Springer pull me up and help me walk away from the scene playing out behind me. My movements feel stiff and robotic. Perhaps I am a robot, devoid of emotion, for how else could I be a part of this?

Springer leads me back to our quarters, for I am unable to do anything aside for numbly walking beside him. He forces me to stop next to the bed and proceeds to strip the clothes from my cold body. I stand there shivering in my underwear while he fetches a cloth and dampens it before returning to gently wipe away the tears racing down my face and the blood staining my skin. When he's finished cleaning me up, he grabs one of his shirts and maneuvers my arms into it, then softly pushes me onto the bed and under the covers.

After he tucks me in, he disappears for a period of time, though I am unable to say how long he is gone. Time has ceased to exist for me. The only thing that seems real is the scene I play over and over in my mind, the stunned disbelief in that child's face as he watched his life bleed out of him. This is what Springer had sheltered me from, what I have never had to face.

When Springer returns, he is showered and freshly dressed. I watch, emotionless, as he drags a chair to my bed and sits down. My eyes track his arm as he reaches over and takes my hand in his warm grip, stroking his fingers in slow circles on my skin. He doesn't say anything, just sits and passes his strength into me through his touch. By slow degrees, I allow myself to come into the present and face the reality of what happened.

Springer watches the transition and says, "I'm so sorry,

Enora. I'm sorry you had to go through that. I never wanted you to have to experience the ugliness first hand. It wasn't supposed to happen like that. I didn't want you to see ..." His voice stops, and I can see a flicker of regret pass across his face. He feels like he let me down, but I have simply been shown the brutal results of my actions.

I squeeze his hand. "I know, Springer. But you can't hide the ugliness from me forever."

He nods, wrapping himself in that control that has enabled him to get through horrors like these countless times before. As I watch him do this, I finally begin to understand the ghosts that he lives with and I feel sadness for the weight of guilt he must feel, for my own is crushing.

I lie silently on the bed while he tells me what occurred in the storage room, how he managed to fight off the man who had tackled him and then dealt with the three others before racing out to find the one who had gotten away. It is clear that while he mentions a man as the person who had knocked him to the ground, he makes no reference to the ages of the others involved. In my heart I know why. He also carefully omits how he 'dealt with' the four infiltrators. I know the tragic end, just not the means.

My eyes begin to feel heavy, as the adrenaline that had kept my heart racing and my muscles taught, leaves my body and exhaustion settles in. The whole ordeal has left me feeling hollowed out and adrift, and I let myself slip into unconsciousness, all too eager to escape reality into dreams. I don't hear Springer leaving to deal with the aftermath of the breach and only know that I have slept when I jolt awake, torn from disturbing dreams.

I sit up and look around the darkness of my room, trying to block the images pummeling my brain. Finally, I quietly make my way to the shower, letting my tears mix with the water, to be sucked down the drain. When the spray of the shower shuts off, I step out and wrap myself in a towel before heading to my room.

I hear quiet footsteps when Springer returns. My door opens, and I turn my head toward his dark shape in the doorway. He walks over and sits on my bed. I don't know what to say. I visualize him pulling the trigger that killed the boy. It is a horrifying scene, but I force myself to face it. How do I feel about what he did? I search my heart and cannot find acceptance.

"How could you do it? They were children, not terrorists." My voice is laced with accusation. Springer reaches over to touch my shoulder, but I flinch, unable to stop myself from recoiling from his touch. He looks different to me now.

His eyes ache at my reaction and he lets out a breath, shoulders slumping in defeat. "Do you think it was easy? Do you have any idea of the guilt I feel?" He turns to me and I can see his eyes rimmed with tears. "I'm a monster." Springer buries his face in his hands, choking on hoarse sobs.

Watching him fall apart, I'm ashamed to have blamed him for what he was trained to do, what he felt he had to do. I know Springer. He was trying to protect me. If I really look at this whole situation, it is Bram whose hand was wrapped around that gun.

"I'm sorry, Springer. It's not your fault." I finally whisper.

Springer turns to me and I open my arms. No more words are needed, as there is nothing that can be said that will erase the awful stain of the night's events.

Time passes quickly and soon dawn is approaching, and with it the harsh reality of an unfinished assignment. I know, without asking, that there was no time for any interrogation. This means that the location of this group of rebels will need to be uncovered through whatever information I can cull from the computer system. I feel the heat of Springer's body penetrate my skin and hear the steady thump of his heart. He is an anchor, both a salvation and a burden. I know I cannot wallow in my misery nor can I simply go rogue with my knowledge. If I did, I would be leaving him at the mercy of the Company. I have no faith that they would see my actions as those of a lone traitor. Their retaliation on Springer is a risk I won't take, one I can't take.

When the first streaks of dawn split the sky, I think how tragic it is that the child who lies cold in some chamber in this monolith will never again see the soft pastels fill the horizon nor the slow rise of the burning sun. I feel Springer shift beneath me and know that it is time to face the day. I pull away and look him in the face, ready to tell him what I know he needs to hear.

"I'm not going anywhere. I won't leave you to do this alone."

Springer's eyes close briefly in relief. "Thank you."

I nod and get up to face the day.

CHAPTER TWENTY-FIVE

By the time we begin our rounds, the events of the previous night are evident to all of the personnel. I note the additional guards and security sweeps of the compound. Springer and I head to our base of operations so that I can delve back into the computer system and try to find the information we need to locate the insurgent group.

As I begin to follow the trail of hacks, my mind starts to wander to the incident during the night, particularly the age of the boy who died in my arms. It strikes me as both risky and odd that children would be used for such a task. Even though my parents were far from doting and affectionate, I can't imagine that they would have allowed me to participate in something that would put my life in eminent danger.

The image of the boy's face flashes across my brain and I am reminded of how frightened he was and how utterly unprepared to cause me any harm. Perhaps it was the pain he felt, having broken his arm in the fall, that made him pause, but I can't help feeling like the whole thing was well beyond his capability or any real training. As I mull it over, other ideas begin to complicate this enigma.

Is this rebel faction predominantly made up of kids?

If so, how could they have survived on their own, with little adult assistance or supervision?

For that matter, how would they even exist if there were no parents to give birth to them?

There must be adults, or is it that this group is a family? Oh, God, were they just a starving family, desperate enough to break into this facility?

I can't begin to go down that path. It's just too awful to consider, so I dismiss it and focus on another scenario. It is plausible that the adults are too frail, or disabled in some way, and must rely on the youth to take charge and gather what they need from these outposts. But then, how did they get here? It's not like this facility is near a town or city. The compound is strategically placed away from civilization as an added layer of security.

I sit up quickly in my chair as my fingers fly across the keys. I know that the building has multiple camera systems in every corridor, aside from sleeping quarters and bathrooms. I also know that the perimeter of the compound is riddled with cameras. I stroke a series of commands onto the keyboard and pull up the video data from the southwest corner of the building. After a moment during which I contemplate the timing of events, I scroll through footage of the area just outside of the fence, hoping to see a vehicle of some sort that would give me a clue as to what direction they had originated from. I slow the video as I get closer to the time when they breach the fence. I can see the point at which the video feed was taken over by a loop for any eyes that were watching but am able to circumvent that and see the real feed. I am dumbfounded when five figures seem to simply coalesce a moderate distance outside the perimeter.

I stop the video and rewind to watch it again, sure that I must have missed something, but it is the same. They just appear. There is no evidence of a vehicle of any kind. *What the hell?* Frustrated by my inability to figure out how they arrived, I rewind the video a third time and slow the feed down so that I can look at it frame by frame.

The video is dark and grainy as I zoom in to the point at which they seem to appear and then I see it, beyond the point at which I saw them enter the section of video I was watching. The ground literally opens and they slip out before it closes again behind them. There is a tunnel system outside the barrier of this facility.

My vision tilts as I take this in. I feel like the images I

am seeing blur with my experiences in Renascence. The tunnels I spent weeks mapping. My assignment to plot the bowels of the city, to look for a resistance that I never really found evidence of. And now I am faced with the very thing I was requisitioned to find in the city, but it is *here*, in an unknown network of tunnels that is nowhere in any data I was given. The correlation is unnerving and once again I feel like an unseen hand is maneuvering me for an unrecognizable purpose. As though my assignment in Renascence was simply training for what I would find here, only it doesn't make any sense. It is maddening.

I lean away from the images on the screen and stretch my neck, hoping to gain some deeper perspective. My eyes drift over to Springer, who is seated in the chair next to me, having fallen asleep after his exertions last night. I have a feeling that he knows more than what he tells me, or what he has permission to tell me. I look back at the screen, at the figures frozen in time.

This tunnel system was not part of the assignment. Should I reveal what I've found? There is only one outcome if I do.

I feel a fissure running through me. On one side is my loyalty to Springer and my family. The other side is my pursuit of the truth and unmasking the face of the DMC. I feel so close to unlocking some essential truth that will help me understand my part in all of this, but I can't grab onto it. There are just too many missing components for me to put it together.

I proceed to watch the footage another couple of times, looking at the indistinct terrain as a small portion of the ground slides inward allowing the individuals to scramble up and out of the opening. At normal film speed, this process actually takes a few seconds leading me to believe that the emerging figures must have been waiting just below the outlet, making it seem as if they just materialize out of nowhere. It is impossible to tell how far the tunnel system may extend but it is plain that it must be a substantial distance as there are no other structures in the vicinity of the compound. In my mind, I start formulating ideas of how the maze of tunnels may snake through the earth and what that could mean as far as their historical significance is concerned. Naturally, I fall back on what I know from Renascence. It's a strange coincidence to be able to use my experiences from that place to try to understand what is going on here. I am lost as to how I am expected to move forward with this.

Springer snores softly and I look over at his face, slack and free of worry in his slumber. I promised him that I would see this through, that I wouldn't abandon him, and this means that I need to show him what I've found and force him to share everything that he knows. No more secrets, no more sheltering me from the realities of what we are a part of. We have come too far now to hide behind fabrications and half-truths.

I nudge his leg a couple of times and he shifts his body before coming awake. His eyes are still ringed with dark circles of exhaustion, but I squelch any guilt and say, "I want to show you something." He yawns and nods, but I am not finished. "After I show you, I need you to tell me anything you've kept hidden from me." I watch as his brow furrows before he slowly gestures his assent.

He scoots forward in his chair after I indicate that I want him to watch the screen. When he's in position, I play the footage at regular speed and watch his face closely for his reaction. I see his look of shock and assume that I must have looked the same.

"Where did they come from?"

"Just watch." I replay it, frame by frame.

His eyebrows shoot up as he watches the ground open and the figures quickly emerge before the earth is sealed, as though nothing had been disturbed. At his request I play it again. He sits back in his chair, eyes still glued to the scene paused on the monitor.

I wait for him to look at me before I ask, "What should we do with this?"

"What do you mean?"

"Springer, don't you feel like we're on the wrong side in all of this?" I pause, needing to choose my words carefully. "From the start, you've shielded me from things, protecting me from whatever you didn't want me to see or know." I watch him carefully, but his face gives nothing away and it's impossible to tell if what I am saying has any impact. "You are always looking out for me, trying to hide the ugliness of what we do. I appreciate you sheltering me from it, but if we are going to get through this together then I need to face the truth. I need to understand my purpose."

He reaches over. "Enora..."

I am not sure what he was about to say because from the corner of my eye I see the monitor go black and then flash before going black again.

"Did you see that?"

He leans in. "Was the video feed cut off or something?"

I shake my head. "No. That was the system resetting itself, but it shouldn't do that on its own."

And then on the black screen we see a cursor illuminate. Both of us are rendered speechless, waiting in anticipation as characters begin to scrawl across the top of the screen.

We know you are there.

Springer and I gasp in shock as the message is completed and then begins to disappear, letter-by-letter. I am about to open my mouth to voice a question, when Springer touches a finger to my lips and points at the screen where another communication is bleeding into the black background.

We know who you are, Enora.

I JUMP OUT OF MY SEAT, KNOCKING INTO SPRINGER. I am pointing to the screen frenziedly, as he looks at me in utter astonishment.

"What the hell is this, Springer? How do they know who I am?"

I can literally see the gears turning in his head as he flips through various responses to determine which reply would be the most appropriate. My temper flares. "Stop it! Stop trying to hide things from me!"

Before he has a chance to react, the message is gone and replaced with a third, more bewildering missive.

We want to meet. It is time for you to learn the truth.

I LOOK AT SPRINGER AND I CAN SEE THAT HE IS weighing the risks. He is always trying to protect me, but I am done being cossetted and sheltered from the reality of the Company. The death of that boy was the final push I needed to accept the fact that I am a killer. It was as though his dead eyes were the mirror I finally held to my face. The reflection I saw is as inescapable as it is horrifying. There is no way for me to ignore the truth, not anymore. There is no return to some fantasy where I am one of the 'good guys.'

As I watch Springer's internal battle play out, I feel my own need for the truth turn into resolution. I coldly decide that if he refuses to join me, then I will go on without him. The twinge of betrayal I feel when I make this decision is quickly smothered. I have to do what is right. It's what my parents would expect of me. It's what I owe Safa. I owe it to myself.

Springer takes a deep breath. "They're right, Enora. It's time you learned the truth."

A rush of profound relief passes through me, along with a twinge of consternation. "Are you admitting that you've kept things from me?"

"Only what I've had to." He grasps my hand and squeezes gently. "We'll do this together."

I nod, my heart beginning to race at the prospect of what this means. We will be taking an irreversible step. Living outside the system, and all that it represents, means no more DMC-provided food, and no water. The Company will hunt us down and I will never see my parents again. These are the costs, and they are steep. But I'm ready.

I see Springer's eyes crinkle slightly as though he has been reading my thoughts, waiting while I come to this decision. His mouth curves in a small smile as he says, "I have so much to tell you."

Let it begin.

AFTERWORD

Enora's story continues in the second installment:

Burden of Truth - On Amazon

Burden of Truth - Other Retailers

ACKNOWLEDGMENTS

The journey of this book has been years long. It is truly a labor of love that began with fragments of ideas that eventually became a coherent story. Its inception began as I researched material I was using for a graduate course that I wrote in Environmental Education. As I read numerous topics regarding the history of the earth to the present, I couldn't help but be struck by the incredible responsibility that humans have with regard to the current state of the planet and its future. Our actions as a species have indisputable repercussions. We are experiencing an array of such consequences today. One critical outcome has been the decline of a common resource in many parts of the world: fresh water. So I began to wonder, what if a drought of unprecedented proportions crept across the globe?

The idea behind the Drought Mitigation Corporation,

or DMC, came from the knowledge that there are always those people who will take advantage of a dire situation for their own gain. I wondered how far such people might go in pursuit of ultimate control and power. I wanted to create an image that truly reflected the belief that power over nature is attainable. Each element in the DMC logo I created has specific meaning.

The triangle is a symbol of earth and the horizontal line is a symbol of water. Across both of these representations is a bold, vertical stripe, which symbolizes power. The completed symbol is the representation of the DMC: power over the land and water. But one has to wonder, can mankind truly have this type of power?

The path a book takes, from the seedlings of ideas to an actual story, is not without numerous helping hands. The four men in my life have been of profound importance and I couldn't have seen this through without their unconditional support. I'm especially grateful for the hours of editing, bottles of wine, chocolate confections, back rubs, and general boy-humor that have helped me get through the ups and downs of the writing process. I am also blessed with friends who have been willing to play the parts of editor, cover designer, and fan club (minus the pompoms). I'm also grateful to my team who believe this unicorn is so magical that she can s*** rainbows. I give a special thank you to Karana for posing as Enora for the cover. Thank you to my editor, David Taylor at theditors.com, you have helped me fulfill my vision.

And to my loving parents who believe I can do anything, even write a book.

ABOUT THE AUTHOR

Kristin Ward is an award-winning young adult author living in Connecticut. A science and math teacher for over twenty years, she infuses her geeky passions into stories that meld realism and fantasy. Kristin embraces her inner nerd regularly, often quoting 80s movies while expecting those around her to chime in with appropriate rejoinders. As a nature freak, she can be found wandering the woods - she may be lost, so please stop and ask if you see her - or chilling in her yard with all manner of furry and feathered friends. Often referred to as a unicorn by colleagues who remain in awe of her ability to create or find various and sundry things in mere moments, in reality, the horn was removed years ago, leaving only a mild imprint that can be seen if she tilts her head just right. A lifelong lover of books and writing, she dreamed of becoming an author for thirty years before publishing her award-winning debut in 2018. Her first novel, **After the Green Withered**, is one of many things you should probably read.

To learn more about the author and read her humorous anecdotes go to: https://www.kristinwardauthor.com/ or follow her on Twitter @KWardAuthor Instagram @Kristin Ward, Author and Facebook @Kristin Ward, Author

Made in the USA
Middletown, DE
21 February 2021